Maiden of the Needle

2

Zeroki

Illustration by
Miho Takeoka

YEN ON
NEW YORK

Maiden of the Needle 2

ZEROKI

TRANSLATION BY KIKI PIATKOWSKA
COVER ART BY MIHO TAKEOKA

This book is a work of fiction. Names, characters, places, and incidents are the product of the author's imagination or are used fictitiously. Any resemblance to actual events, locales, or persons, living or dead, is coincidental.

HARIKO NO OTOME Vol.2
©Zeroki 2021
First published in Japan in 2021 by KADOKAWA CORPORATION, Tokyo.
English translation rights arranged with KADOKAWA CORPORATION, Tokyo through TUTTLE-MORI AGENCY, INC., Tokyo.

English translation © 2023 by Yen Press, LLC

Yen Press, LLC supports the right to free expression and the value of copyright. The purpose of copyright is to encourage writers and artists to produce the creative works that enrich our culture.

The scanning, uploading, and distribution of this book without permission is a theft of the author's intellectual property. If you would like permission to use material from the book (other than for review purposes), please contact the publisher. Thank you for your support of the author's rights.

Yen On
150 West 30th Street, 19th Floor
New York, NY 10001

Visit us at yenpress.com | facebook.com/yenpress | twitter.com/yenpress
yenpress.tumblr.com | instagram.com/yenpress

First Yen On Edition: September 2023
Edited by Yen On Editorial: Rachel Mimms
Designed by Yen Press Design: Liz Parlett

Yen On is an imprint of Yen Press, LLC.
The Yen On name and logo are trademarks of Yen Press, LLC.

The publisher is not responsible for websites (or their content) that are not owned by the publisher.

Library of Congress Cataloging-in-Publication Data
Names: Zeroki, author. | Takeoka, Miho, illustrator. | Piatkowska, Kiki, translator.
Title: Maiden of the needle / Zeroki ; illustration by Miho Takeoka ; translation by Kiki Piatkowska.
Other titles: Hariko no otome. English
Description: First Yen On edition. | New York, NY : Yen On, 2023–
Identifiers: LCCN 2022057331 | ISBN 9781975361624 (v. 1 ; trade paperback) | ISBN 9781975361648 (v. 2 ; trade paperback)
Subjects: CYAC: Fantasy. | Reincarnation—Fiction. | Sewing—Fiction. | LCGFT: Fantasy fiction. | Light novels.
Classification: LCC PZ7.1.Z48 Mai 2023 | DDC [Fic]—dc23
LC record available at https://lccn.loc.gov/2022057331

ISBNs: 978-1-9753-6164-8 (paperback)
978-1-9753-6165-5 (ebook)

10 9 8 7 6 5 4 3 2 1

LSC-C

Printed in the United States of America

Maiden of the Needle

2

Contents

CHAPTER 1	The Changing of Seasons	003
CHAPTER 2	Moving House	009
CHAPTER 3	Portal	037
CHAPTER 4	Schnell	067
CHAPTER 5	Apprenticeship	087
INTERLUDE	A Monstrous Spider	103
CHAPTER 6	An Unexpected Connection	111
CHAPTER 7	Sacred Tree	125
CHAPTER 8	And Then	143
EXCLUSIVE SHORT STORY 1	Playing in the Snow and an Amulet	149
EXCLUSIVE SHORT STORY 2	Love at First Sight for a Mermaid	159
BONUS	Character Artwork	169

Characters

Protagonists

Yui Nuir
A Japanese teenager reborn as a highly gifted seamstress who possesses faysight, the ability to see fairies. Unaware of her talents, her family treated her with scorn. Meeting Rodin and Argit changed her life dramatically for the better.

Argit Lomestometlo
The previous king. Upon recognizing Yui's genius, he proposed marriage in order to protect her.

Calostira Household

Rodin Calostira
A second-rank noble serving at the royal court. Smitten by the beauty of Yui's needlework, he employed her as his own seamstress and later introduced her to Argit.

Endelia
Rodin's housekeeper. Quiet, but terrifying when angered, she's the household's "big sister" figure. Has a dark fairy who dresses like a cat.

Luroo Loulouoo
A certified physician who works for Rodin as a maid and nurse. She looks after Yui, who is of very weak constitution.

Senri Kamioka
Works for Rodin as a maid. Looks like an ordinary village girl, but has the strength of a giant. Her freckles add to her charm.

Linne
An older woman employed by the Calostira household as a seamstress. Oversees Yui after she moved to Rodin's residence.

Argit's Attendants and Yui's Protectors

Stolle Menes
Argit's personal guard and the only daughter of House Menes, the nation's chief military advisors. Yui's blessweaving awoke Stolle's armor fairy, granting her magical protection. Stolle and Rodin had been friends since their school days and are now a couple.

Mimachi
Argit's cheerful maid. The life of every party. Obsessed with cute girls, always trying to get her wandering hands on Yui.

The Royal Family

Amnart Lomestometlo
Argit's son and the current king. His engagement to Hania was officially announced at the last royal ball. Has a high-level green fairy.

Nobles Close to the Royals

Hania Furke
The eldest daughter of House Furke, a family of artisan dyers. A first-rate martial artist who fights with fiery knuckledusters that are imbued with the power of her high-level flame fairy.

Toluamia Mishutu
A first-rank noble serving as the military's magical advisor. Has been friends with Rodin, Stolle, and Amnart since they were in school.

Meilia Nuir
Yui's younger sister. Was once a very timid little girl who adored Yui, but her parents' bad influence turned her into an uppity young lady with nothing but contempt for her sister.

Fairies

The Realm Weaveguardian
The Lomestometlo Kingdom's guardian fairy, created by Ariadne and the founder of House Nuir. Under a curse cast by the previous queen, Lestlana.

Ariadne
A spider monster who made a pact with the founder of House Nuir. Created a nation where the Nuir pact bearer and the first kings could coexist with fairies to keep the realm safe. Like Yui, she transmigrated from Japan. Her wish is to be freed from the life of a monster, which can only happen when Yui's spider evolves into a divine beast.

Purple Prince
A dark fairy and one of Yui's familiars. Looks like a boy, which is unusual for a fairy.

Moontide Fairy
One of Yui's guardian fairies. Has bunny ears. Offers protective blessings of moon and water affinities.

Tree Fairy
One of Yui's guardian fairies. Wears a flower crown. The very first fairy Yui healed.

Others

Lestlana
Argit's second wife whose morbid jealousy cursed the Realm Weaveguardian. After Argit divorced her, she was banished from the kingdom and forced to return to her home country. Her curse continues to plague the Realm Weaveguardian to this day.

The Story So Far

After her short life in Japan, Tsumugi was reincarnated into another world as Yui Nuir. Born with the gift of faysight, she could see fairies and magic. With fairies as her playmates, Yui learned how to wield magic.

When she turned ten, her parents gave her a spider, as the family trade was blessweaving: the magical craft of imbuing spider silk with magic to sew garments with magical effects.

Having done handicrafts in her previous life as a hobby, Yui could sew beautifully and with astonishing speed—but she used non-magical thread for her needlework, since she didn't know about blessweaving. Consequently, her parents deemed her inept at the family craft, treating her with scorn and abuse.

Then, at age fifteen, Yui moved to the residence of the second-rank noble Rodin Calostira to work for him as a seamstress. He welcomed her with warmth she had never experienced. To repay him for his kindness, she made scented sachets for his household, using the blessweaving technique for the very first time. Rodin discovered that the sachets were blesswoven and realized Yui's talent was on par with the founder of House Nuir. He promptly arranged for her to meet Argit Lomestometlo, the previous king.

Argit saw how close Yui was with the fairies, who freely assisted her as she sewed. He knew that her amazing talent put her at great risk—her family would desperately want to get her back into their clutches to exploit her. In order to prevent that, he proposed marriage to Yui and nominated her as the next head of House Nuir. While Yui was surprised by this unexpected development, she quickly understood Argit's motives and accepted his proposal.

Their engagement was announced at a ball at the royal palace, and it was there that Yui met a special fairy, the Realm Weaveguardian. This fairy's left arm was burned and festering from a curse placed on her by Argit's morbidly jealous second wife. Left untreated, the curse might corrupt the entire kingdom.

Hoping it would help her cure the Realm Weaveguardian, Yui sought to make a pact with the House Nuir founder's spider monster. She was surprised to find out that this spider—Ariadne—had lived in Japan in her past life, too. Ariadne explained that she was the one who created the Realm Weaveguardian, and that the curse could only be banished after cutting off the fairy's arm with a wind-property weapon.

With Yui's successful installation as the new head of House Nuir, she and Argit begin their quest to save the Realm Weaveguardian.

CHAPTER 1

The Changing of Seasons

Had I ever noticed the changing of seasons since my rebirth in this world? Not while I was living at the Nuir family residence, at least, where the seasons seemed to be largely the same. The climate was rather cool year-round, although I wasn't allowed to leave the house back then, so that was just my impression from the inside. In my previous world, Japan had four distinct seasons, and there were tropical islands where it was summer all year. I had to wonder whether this world even had different seasons.

I was wrong, though—spring, summer, fall, and winter did exist in this world, but the concept of seasons didn't apply in exactly the same way.

The day after the battle at the royal palace, I was told I'd be moving in with Argit. Apparently, summer was about to start in the area where Rodin lived.

There were twelve months in a year, seven days in a week, and twenty-four hours in a day, just like in my original world—because it was created by a person from that same world, as Aria told me. Except some things were completely different.

"Summer is coming...?"

"Ah, you don't know about seasons, do you?" Rodin said to me. "They don't change in the region you're from. Well, we say it's summer when the weather gets very hot."

"The weather..."

Whoa, this was exactly how people talked about summer in my old world. My eyes widened in surprise.

"It's one of the terms we use to describe local climates. The Nuirs live in an autumnal region, but here after spring we have summer."

"Autumn...and spring...?"

"It's tricky; the two are quite similar. The temperature is moderate during both, but autumn is a little cooler, while spring is slightly on the warmer side."

I was confused. The Nuir residence was only a couple days' coach ride from Rodin's. Looking at a map, it was no different from traveling from one prefecture in Japan to the next. I had noticed that it seemed warmer where Rodin lived, but I wouldn't have guessed that the two locations were experiencing entirely different seasons.

Rodin's residence was a few hours from the royal palace, which was like traveling from the countryside to the capital of the same prefecture.

"Winter, meanwhile, is the opposite of summer. We say it's winter in places which are very cold, or which become very cold for some part of the year."

"Spring, summer, autumn, winter..."

"The doctor says the summertime climate is detrimental to your health. It's not good for your fairy familiars, either. Your dark fairy is in a class of his own, but you don't have any other high-level fairies, and all the common ones have better affinity with spring and winter. Fairies' power wanes when

the season doesn't suit them, which could make you feel low on energy, and in the worst-case scenario, you might even fall ill. That's what happened to Argit, so we can reasonably assume it would apply to you, as well. That's why you should move elsewhere before summer arrives here."

The region with the royal palace and Rodin's residence had spring for half of the year and summer in the second half. The abrupt change in temperature, which to me with my past life memories seemed very unnatural, was apparently the effect of local fairies and magic. That also explained how places that weren't very far apart could have different climates.

Humans with high-level fairy familiars weren't affected by the changes in temperature, but those with low-level fairies would become unwell the moment the season didn't suit their familiars. When Argit's fairies had used their magic to help the Realm Weaveguardian, they reverted to low levels, and he almost died when summer began in the capital.

Basically, Argit could no longer withstand summer temperatures, and I was supposedly of the same constitution.

"So, although it's a little early, you'll be moving to the house where you and Argit will be living after getting married."

I thought about how after this marriage, I'd be leaving Rodin's residence for good… It made me sad. My emotions must have shown on my face, because everyone started saying that I was welcome to visit every spring.

In six months, when the summer ended and spring returned, I would be getting married to Argit, and Hania to Amnart. With that done, we were going to banish the kingdom's curse once and for all.

For as long as I could, I tried not to think about having to leave Rodin's house, or about my marriage.

I was moving to a city called Menesmetlo, which had labyrinths. The city was within land belonging to Stolle's family. For half a year it was spring there—which overlapped with spring in Rodin's area—but for the other half, it was winter.

Other locations had been suggested, but Argit chose Menesmetlo for three reasons. The seasons, and especially winter, suited both me and Argit. The labyrinth the city was known for was of the wind element. Wind labyrinths were exceedingly rare, and only two in total were known of in the country. Mountain Peak Labyrinth was the other one, and true to its name, it was on a mountain peak, in a region very far from Rodin's residence where we wouldn't be able to stay very long.

We needed both the magic of a high-level wind fairy and a powerful weapon to sever the Realm Weaveguardian's cursed arm before we could heal her. So far, we didn't know anyone who might possess such a fairy familiar, or an appropriate weapon. Argit's connections were searching for any adventurers within the kingdom who might be able to help, but we might have better luck finding our fairy and weapon in the dungeon. It would also be good practice before the battle with the curse.

The third reason for choosing Menesmetlo was that Argit had a retirement residence there—one of several. We wouldn't be staying there, though. Instead, our home for the next half of the year would be a secret—but not hidden—residence belonging to House Menes.

Argit and his party had half a year to train for the final battle, to find a severance-effect labyrinth weapon, and to find a high-level wind fairy—or to recruit helpful adventurers with that kind of weapon and that kind of fairy.

A house near the labyrinth would be our base of operations until we fulfilled those objectives.

CHAPTER 2

Moving House

And so, only two days after the royal ball, I departed Rodin's residence among heartfelt farewells and well-wishes for my engagement.

Leaving these people—the first people I'd grown close to in this world—had me crying my eyes out. The last time I cried that much was when I was only a baby. The memories of everything from my past life, now gone forever—my friends, my workplace, and so many others—had become unbearable.

My thoughts went on a tangent, and I remembered that I never got to say good-bye to the person who'd tutored me at the Nuir residence. Come to think of it, she was the first person in this world who I became somewhat close with. She left when my parents decided I was useless and inept. I hadn't had the time to be sad; everything had happened so fast, it didn't feel real—the next thing I knew, I was basically a slave.

The tutor protested to my parents, appalled by how they were treating me, which resulted in her getting fired. I was actually relieved that she

wouldn't have anything to do with my family anymore, but my eyes filled with fresh tears when I imagined how sad she must have been.

"Are you all right, Yui?"

Argit had come to get me. When he saw me crying, he lifted me into his arms with a sympathetic smile.

"Sorry to take you away from somewhere so important to you."

"That's…okay. We'll all…see each other…again."

"That's right."

Even if it weren't for Argit, Rodin would have had to send me away for the summer season because of my weak constitution. Argit really had nothing to apologize for, but he looked at me sadly, gently stroking my hair.

Although I was in low spirits, the journey to Argit's home was drastically more comfortable than the ride from the Nuir home to Rodin's residence.

The roads were bad in the Nuir territory, so the carriage shook terribly. My family forced me to work right up to the very moment I left, so I started my journey hungry and tired after a sleepless night. It was my first time in a horse-drawn vehicle, too. Being knocked around as the carriage made its progress on the road made me lose the last of my energy; I ended up passed out for the most of the trip.

My memories of it were so hazy—I couldn't remember how many days it took, but later, I was told it was only a day and a half. The roads hadn't always been so riddled with potholes, but they had fallen into disrepair when my indolent grandfather took over as the head of the family. Also, the carriage was falling apart.

The horse-drawn carriage Argit had prepared for us seemed simple at a glance, but its performance was top class. I was promised the ride would be so smooth on any terrain that I'd be able to knit during the journey without feeling sick. Despite its considerable size, the carriage was lighter than the coach I had traveled in before, and it seemed sturdier, too.

To give a better idea of the size, it was like the four-horse carriages used by wealthy merchants, except that this one was easily pulled by only two horses.

The coachman, Gogol, was very excited to drive it, loudly oohing and aahing, unable to sit still for a while. He was like a gearhead driving his dream car...even though to me, this looked just like an ordinary merchant's carriage.

The journey to our new home took us three days. Summer was just beginning when we left Rodin's, but a mere two-day journey later, the air became chilly, and the leaves on trees were in shades of red. We'd skipped over summer, going from spring directly to fall.

Also, we stayed overnight at several inns, while the journey to Rodin's had been nonstop.

While outside, I wore a wide-brimmed hat with a lacy trim which hid most of my face. Being seen wasn't a problem for me when I went shopping before my transformation, since I still had that starved child look about me. Now, though, I was strictly forbidden from venturing out alone. I was textbook jailbait, after all.

Actually, this was my first time staying at an inn in this world. The food was delicious: We had offal stew, and also something like...udon? It was similar to the *houtou* udon miso stew from Yamanashi. My first Japanese-style meal in this new life—what a comfort!

I also got to eat raw egg on rice! We passed through a town where there was a custom of eating eggs raw. I hadn't eaten anything like that since my reincarnation.

Once, in my previous life, I was talking to my friend about egg on rice, and I realized I'd never tried it. When I went back home, I made some just

for myself in secret, and it tasted amazing. The egg on rice I had at this inn brought back touching memories of how delicious that simple meal I'd eaten all by my lonesome was.

Not all the food I had during this journey was familiar, though. There was a stew with potatoes and some sort of melt-in-your-mouth cubed meat…which I was later told wasn't meat at all, but fish! I could've sworn it was pork! Apparently, it's pretty tricky to make, since overcooking the fish makes it fall to pieces. This particular fish came from a large nearby lake.

In this world, I had been eating mostly food similar to European cuisine, so it felt fresh to have Japanese-style dishes. Or I guess izakaya-style, should I say? It was the sort of food my friend's mom would make—the flavors of homemade food cooked by a loving mother. Not my mother, though—my family meals were very stressful, and I didn't even remember what they tasted like. My father always complained about the food, and my mother—who was dead set on trying to please him—wasn't able to tweak her cooking to his liking, which meant she probably wasn't a skilled cook.

In any case, I now understood why Aria was so passionate about cooking and trying new cuisines. It was only after eating her cake that I realized my sense of taste hadn't been working properly until then; maybe the cake healed me? The meals at Rodin's were tasty, but I wasn't able to fully appreciate the flavors before Aria gave me that cake. The Nuirs fed me scraps (when they felt caring enough to feed me at all), and they tasted so awful, I developed something of a mental block for food to cope. According to the doctor, I survived in my emaciated state only owing to the fairies pouring their magic into my food and drink.

After having such limited culinary experiences, Argit made this something of a gourmet discovery trip for me. I suspected he changed our itinerary just so that we could stop by more interesting eateries. There were so many fruits and vegetables unique to the locations we were passing by. It started feeling fun, like I was on a vacation.

We arrived in Menesmetlo on schedule, three days after our departure from Rodin's. Gogol said we'd never have made it that quickly if it weren't for Argit's special carriage.

"I doubt it's the carriage, considering how quickly we got here," Argit said, visibly confused.

Personally, I thought Gogol was the one responsible for our speedy trip. I'd noticed fairies hovering near the horses' hooves and the carriage wheels every now and again, although I couldn't tell whether they were doing the work.

Gogol spoke with an accent similar to the fearsomely strong maid Senri. He was also one of the few members of Rodin's household who didn't have any fairy familiars with him despite being well-liked by fairies. Whenever Senri wielded her might, fairies would quietly appear out of nowhere around her. I surmised something similar was going on with Gogol when he was driving.

Menesmetlo was almost as big as the royal capital, densely packed with buildings and a high population. Besides the labyrinth, it was also famous for its hot springs. It attracted a lot of visitors, even from abroad, and consequently, many of the buildings we were passing by were inns.

The local architecture featured roofs slanted at sharp angles. I was told it was so snow would slide off them, rather than pile up and risk crushing the roofs. Narrow street gutters with steaming hot water were running alongside the main roads to keep them clear of snow.

Our new abode, the secret Menes family retreat, was in the residential area near a labyrinth.

"Oh!"

Oddly enough, it was cylindrical. If somebody had told me it was an old castle tower that got chopped off several decades ago, I'd have believed it. Among the rectangular houses with their slanted roofs, this one stood out like a sore thumb.

The cool weather was more autumnal than wintry, which was why the vines creeping up half of this brick tower had yellow and red foliage, softening the look of this otherwise austere, quaint gray structure.

"It's…secret," I said, "but not…hidden…"

Mimachi burst out laughing at my comment. Stolle hung her head, unable to say anything in defense of this strange tower.

At least it was true that nobody would suspect this to be a secret getaway of the nobles ruling this territory. The lords who would sometimes stay in the tower could easily pass for adventurers rather than aristocrats.

I would be staying in the tower while Argit and his party explored the labyrinth, but this didn't mean I'd be lazing around with nothing to do.

First of all, I had to make outfits for my wedding in six months' time. I also had to sew garments that would protect Argit's party from the monster the curse would manifest as. Then there was the matter of purifying gloves for the cursed Realm Weaveguardian. I'd have to make many—as many as I could. Between all these tasks, I didn't really have time to sit around doing nothing.

Argit's party included Stolle and Mimachi. Amnart and Hania possessed high-level guardian fairies, such as Hania's flame fairy, who could vanquish curses, so they joined the party despite the dangers. I felt responsible for making blesswoven garments to keep them safe.

I was very quick with needlework, but I hadn't had much experience with blessweaving yet. My plan was to make as many garments as I could, including gloves for the Realm Weaveguardian, to hone my skills.

My priority was to get in a bit of exercise to boost my stamina.

The Realm Weaveguardian kept our kingdom safe, so any curse affecting her would also be detrimental to our country. For now, the curse was still being kept in check, thanks to Argit's little guardian fairies. He'd told me these fairies had sacrificed most of their power to stop the ill effects of the Realm Weaveguardian's curse.

Apparently, they used to be mid- to high-level. I thought they must have been very fond of Argit to give up so much of their magic that they shrank back to the size of baby fairies.

Several other people agreed to help Argit in battle at his request: for example, the magician Toluamia Mishutu, who contained Aria's labyrinth in a magic circle to stop it from consuming the entire palace. A first-rank noble himself, he'd been friends with Rodin and Stolle since they were schoolchildren, and he currently worked as the military's magecraft advisor. He was going to join Argit after wrapping up some other assignment.

Another person who joined us was Endelia, Rodin's housekeeper. She and the cook, Mijit, arrived at our temporary home ahead of everyone else to get the place ready. I was surprised when I was told she'd be fighting, too.

Endelia had a high-level dark fairy as her familiar. I'd always sensed the fairy's presence, but I'd never seen it at Rodin's residence. It turned out the fairy had been hiding in Endelia's shadow. Come to think of it, Purple Prince was also hiding in my shadow most of the time. Maybe it was just what dark fairies did.

Wait... If Purple Prince can cut through blesswoven fabric, maybe he can also unravel the curse?

I looked at him questioningly, and he crossed his hands to form an X. I

sensed he was trying to tell me that he was able to do it, but there were reasons he couldn't.

Because it would unravel the Realm Weaveguardian at the same time?

He nodded.

Whoa, freaky!

Hold on… Purple Prince is really tiny, probably a low-level fairy, maybe close to becoming mid-level…

B-but he seriously can unravel her?

Boy fairies were very rare. Or, to be precise, I had never seen any besides Purple Prince. I should've asked Aria about that before she went back to sleep. Maybe he was a very special kind of fairy?

…Anyway, getting back on topic: Endelia used to be a maid-bodyguard at the royal palace, and she was incredibly strong, apparently.

It was all quite mysterious. At present, these were the members of Argit's party:

Argit.

Stolle and Mimachi.

Amnart and Hania.

Toluamia and Endelia.

The captain of the royal guard and the elderly butler who'd joined the party last time, although I didn't know much about them.

Hania's older brother, who was supposedly fearsomely strong.

And a few others, since we were expecting this battle to be huge. They all had half a year to train and prepare.

We were also hoping to recruit someone with a severance-effect weapon and someone with a guardian fairy. It wasn't just our small group looking for adventurers who would fit the bill—the search was being carried out nationwide. But neither owners of magic weapons nor those blessed with a wind-property guardian fairy could be lured with mere promise of honor and status. If anything, that was more likely to be a deterrent. That's why the reward offered was a blesswoven garment made by me.

◆

When we arrived at the Menes family's secret house, Stolle first wanted to show me to the cellar. The coachman Gogol and Mijit the beastkin were going to unpack my belongings.

"I hope you enjoy it," Argit said to me.

"Enjoy...?" I replied.

Enjoy what? I wondered.

"There's something special in the cellar that I think you might like, Lady Yui."

We walked down the stone staircase, which led us to a changing room. The interior was modest but quite big.

"The best thing about this house lies ahead. It's an underground hot spring."

"Gyuh, Stolle! Let go of my face! I have to accompany Lady Yui as her personal maid! It's my duty!"

"Don't worry, Mimachi. Endelia will accompany her on this occasion."

Stolle restrained Mimachi and dragged her out of the changing room.

"The ride in His Highness's carriage was no doubt comfortable, but aren't you tired from being on the road? Relax in the hot spring before dinner and take it easy for the rest of the day," said Endelia, walking into the room with a change of clothes in a basket, as Mimachi's protests died away in the background.

Meanwhile, Senri kept the door to the changing room shut. She worked as a maid for Rodin, and her manners were impeccable for a commoner. We got along right away. Rodin loaned her to us so that she would look after me.

Senri was an ordinary human, but she was the strongest of us all. Even Mimachi, who could break open pretty much any door, couldn't get in when Senri was holding it shut.

With access to the changing room closely guarded, Endelia quickly helped me take off my clothes and put on a bathing suit. I could get changed without help, but with Mimachi being a constant threat, it had been decided someone should help to make it quicker.

My nurse, Luroo, changed into a bathing suit as well. She took my hand and walked with me to the hot spring, making sure I wouldn't slip and fall. Past the changing room was a warm, steam-filled limestone cave.

"A hot spring..."

But let's not forget it was a different world. The cave walls were covered in some sort of bellflowers, which emitted a faint white glow. It really looked magical.

"So...pretty."

An underground hot spring!

"The nearby labyrinth's magic reaches this hot spring, Lady Yui."

"S-Stolle?!"

I was so captivated by my surroundings that I hadn't noticed that Stolle had followed us inside. She'd always had to wait outside when I was bathing, restraining Mimachi, so I wasn't expecting to see her. And I certainly wasn't expecting to see her without her armor. She'd changed into a camisole-like bathing suit, just like everyone else. Talk about a rare sight! She had an amazing body.

The bathing suits in this world were made from some unusual fabric which didn't stick to skin when wet. They were unaffected by water resistance, which made them perfect for bathing, but at the same time, they were very thin. Even without getting wet, these garments were pretty much see-through.

And that's what Stolle, with her incredibly fit body, was wearing.

I could guess people's sizes at a glance, although actually seeing what someone looked like under their clothes was different. Stolle was busty, but thanks to her physical training, there was no sagging. No one would've guessed that she used to bind her breasts until I made her armor more comfortable.

But if Stolle isn't standing guard, who's keeping Mimachi away...?

Before I could ask, I heard Mimachi whining.

"Nuh-oh-oh! Endelia, please! Don't make your fairy blind me! I can't see anything!"

There she was, walking unsteadily, arms flailing, with a big purple cat sitting on her head—Endelia's high-level dark fairy. And by cat, I meant this was a female human-shaped fairy in a cat costume. Why, I had no idea. She was as big as my torso, which would be really big for a cat. She was biting Mimachi's head, dangling over her face. Her tail was connected by a magical thread to Endelia, whose magic made the fairy fluff up like a dark cloud, blinding Mimachi—that explained why Mimachi was crying out helplessly.

Endelia was close behind; she'd never bathed with me before, either. Actually, neither had Mimachi! Normally, Stolle and Endelia would be keeping her away, so that she wouldn't get up to any mischief.

And wow, check out Endelia... She was sexy even in an ordinary maid outfit, but in nothing but a thin bathing suit, she was sexual dynamite!

It was the first time I'd seen Mimachi in a bathing suit, too. She looked just like I had imagined.

For some reason, Endelia appeared bustier than Stolle, even though I was sure they were the same size. I was confident in my seamstress's eye for sizing.

...She couldn't possibly have gotten less *busty.*

Senri came in next, covering her breasts with a blank look in her eyes.

Yep. She can't help comparing herself to the other ladies, huh?

Oh, I figured out why Endelia's bust seemed bigger—it was the contrast with Mimachi, who was standing off to the side in front of her.

I was impressed not just by Endelia's physique, but also by her control of magic. She didn't let even a molecule of her magic escape from her body. Without perfect, conscious control of one's magic, a small trickle of it escapes continuously. Some people didn't emanate magic at all because of health conditions, but that wasn't the case with Endelia. She was probably nearly as good at controlling it as I was.

I based my assessment on the fact that Endelia's magic connected seamlessly with her fairy's tail, without losing shape and drifting off in cotton candy puffs. Her thread of magic was also thinner than what I'd seen magicians like Toluamia produce. Toluamia's magical thread was as thick as a man's arm, while Endelia's was like a little girl's—the same girth as the dark feline fairy's tail. The fairy wrapped her tail around it, not minding this magical leash.

Endelia noticed me looking at the stumbling Mimachi. She smiled and whispered, "Even if she can't see, the earth fairies will help her get around."

Mimachi was treading hesitantly, her body shimmering with a faint magical glow. I'd observed that before in people who used magic to augment their natural strength. I thought about how she conjured a large number of pillars in the last battle. She couldn't possibly have had enough magic to make that many. How did she do that?

"Earth fairies…?" I wondered aloud.

"The earth fairies assist Mimachi with a little bit of their magic when she touches earth or rocks with her bare skin," Stolle explained. "It's a special trait of people of her race."

"Special trait…?"

"Yes. The Terra have a very high affinity with earth fairies."

Stolle took my hand and pulled me away from the incoming Mimachi.

"As long as there's soil or rocks she can touch, she can conjure rock pillars or sense where people are standing. She can't crack through labyrinth walls or floors, though."

Stolle made me twirl around, escaping Mimachi's reach as if we were performing a dance. It was true that even without being able to see us, Mimachi knew exactly where we were. Stolle skillfully maneuvered me so that I kept dodging Mimachi, without it tiring me out. The next thing I knew, I was laughing out loud.

"Wow!" I cried. "I'm...dancing!"

"Stop it, Stolle! No fair!" Mimachi whined.

"No, you stop following Lady Yui!"

Stolle spun me in another pirouette, when suddenly, there was a loud *thud*. Before I knew it, I was in Luroo's arms, and Stolle, who'd let go of me, was grinning.

"Also, Mimachi's race is very tough. She can smash into the wall without suffering any damage."

I've seen that happen many times.

"Mimachi, you'll have to get that wall fixed," said Endelia.

"You two are so mean to me!"

Huh, she does *seem just fine.*

No matter how many times I witnessed Mimachi smashing into walls, it still shocked me.

Dancing was common practice among the nobility, and I, too, had been taught the basics when I was little...but I'd forgotten them all. If it weren't for Stolle's careful leading, I'd have tripped over my own feet. Each pirouette made my bathing suit flare out like the skirt of a dress, and it looked very pretty.

I liked to think up designs for dresses that would look nice when dancing, but it didn't seem like I'd have enough stamina to dance myself in the near future.

By the way, I had made the bathing suit I was wearing. I used more fabric than usual, but I carefully designed it to make it easy to wash me. Regular bathing suits were just like long shirts, and it was very difficult to wash a person with that on.

Before my engagement, I was considered a child, and the maids would wash me while I was naked. Once I was betrothed, though, it was considered inappropriate for anyone, even other women, to see me unclothed.

At the Nuirs', the maids would just dunk me in a cold bath with my regular clothes on…

Commoners always bathed in the nude, apparently. Some aristocratic customs really didn't make sense. The maids see me naked when they help me get changed; why go through all the trouble of keeping me clothed in the bath?

Getting bathed while wearing a regular bathing suit was the height of inconvenience. The maid helping me would uncover a small part of my body, wash it, cover it up, uncover another bit to wash… So I made my own, which covered the bust and the hips, but had long slits on the sides for easy access. I added more layers to it for further coverage. It worked really well thanks to how lightweight the fabric was.

The dresses I saw other ladies wear at the ball looked terribly heavy with many layers piled on. They'd be better off in something light, which would emphasize the beauty of their movement when they danced…

While I was lost in thought, pondering dress designs, Luroo carried me to a chair with a bucket next to it, where she was going to wash me first.

"The wall doesn't need fixing anyhow! It's part of the labyrinth, so it didn't get cracked or anything!"

Mimachi had peeled herself off the wall and was chasing Stolle, who kept gracefully evading her.

"If this is the best you can do, you need to train more," said Stolle.

"She won't catch anyone if she can't sense shifts in body weight," Luroo added.

Luroo was my nurse, and a qualified physician. She had blue hair and a warm personality. She was the one usually tasked with bathing me, from when I first arrived at Rodin's residence, through the period of acute growing pains, and onward. I heard she was older than Endelia, but she looked maybe two or three years older than Senri. She was a caring, lovable beauty.

Luroo started washing my hair, chatting pleasantly with Endelia, who was scrubbing me down.

"Fwahhh..."

They worked quickly, and soon I was covered in soap bubbles. Endelia never washed me at Rodin's, since our schedules didn't match up. She was quicker and gentler than anyone else, which made the experience quite pleasant. I felt warm and relaxed from head to toe.

"Ahhh..."

Luroo lifted me onto her lap to keep my feet off the ground. She rinsed my hair, and Endelia rinsed the bubbles off my body, following up with a massage. It was heavenly.

"This bathing suit is excellent. It's so easy to wash you."

This was my first time wearing it. I had it in my travel bag all along, but the inns provided bathing suits for the guests, so I had been using them instead. Endelia's praise motivated me.

"I'll make more...for everyone."

"Hee-hee, much obliged, Lady Yui," Luroo said gently. "I'm sure it would take you no time at all with how fast you are, but no sewing today."

"?"

Moving House

"As part of your convalescence, I'm going to teach you to swim. Swimming is an excellent way to strengthen the body without too much exertion. We're going to take it easy today; you must be tired from traveling. I'm sure you'll fall asleep as soon as your head hits the pillow after dinner."

Yeah, I've been doing a lot of that lately...

Trying not to think about how weak I was, I gazed at the hot spring, so vast it was more of a subterranean lake. Wouldn't swimming in hot water give me a head rush? It didn't seem like the best idea.

"Oh, don't worry. The water to our right is quite warm, but the temperature drops the farther out you go."

Endelia pointed toward a huge crystal pillar in the middle of the hot spring. It looked so fantastical, it took my breath away.

"It gets deep very quickly past that pillar. Don't get too close."

"Aw..."

I was sorely disappointed to hear that.

"My, you'd like to see it up close?" asked Luroo.

"That should be fine as long as Luroo goes with you," said Endelia.

"With...Luroo?"

"She's a mermaid. Water's her element."

"You have nothing to worry about, Endelia! Besides, Lady Yui has a water fairy with her. We mermaids can sense water-affinity fairies. Lady Yui's seems to have another affinity mixed in as well. A complementary one, I suppose?"

Luroo motioned with her hands toward where my Moontide Fairy was hovering. "The heat seems to bother her, but she must be well suited to this region. She's gotten much stronger," Luroo muttered.

More importantly...

"You're a mermaid!"

Mermaids were real in this world! I never expected that someone I knew personally would turn out to be one. From what I'd read about the merfolk, they were the third rarest race, most likely to be encountered in coastal areas. Their way of life was different from the land dwellers, so they supposedly never settled on land…

It suddenly struck me that I'd never asked anyone about their races. Better late than never, I suppose?

"On land, we're indistinguishable from humans."

Right. I certainly couldn't tell she was a mermaid just from looking at her.

"Mimachi has Terra blood in her. I'm a demon," said Endelia.

"Wow!"

Endelia's a demon! That…makes a lot of sense, actually.

The demons had a country of their own, where the king was chosen by a powerful magical sword. Compared to the other races, the demons had many amazing abilities, and they were famous for their seductive beauty. They used to live on another continent, but it sank to the bottom of the ocean. All of it except for the demon nation, which drifted to our continent together with its inhabitants. Or at least, that's what the legends said.

The demon kingdom was a prosperous land inhabited mostly by demons, who were reluctant to move out to other countries. Going on a trip was one thing, but it was almost unheard of for any of them to move abroad permanently.

Then again, if Luroo, a mermaid, was working as a nursemaid, maybe I shouldn't have been so shocked that Endelia, a demon, was a housekeeper? Other maids told me that she used to work at the royal palace before taking up her position at Rodin's residence, but they didn't know much more about her besides that. The reason for her job change was some annoyingly persistent man who kept pursuing her. Rodin came across them one time,

Moving House

when the man was badgering her, and drove him away. She then offered to work for him as a maid.

"...Lady Yui, nothing seems to faze you," Endelia commented. "You're so stoic."

"In fairness, it'd be more surprising if Endelia was an ordinary human," said Luroo.

"I'm the only common-born human in this group," Senri noted.

She did, at least superficially, look like a commoner. She had golden-brown hair, freckles, and eyes so dark they were almost black, like most Japanese people. Maybe that's why we became friends right away.

"You may look like an ordinary human commoner, Senri, but I'm sure you have some giantess blood in you," Endelia teased.

Maybe she was right. I'd seen Senri easily carry a heavy wooden chest that Gogol and Mijit were struggling to lift together.

Giants weren't just rare—they were one of the three mythical races. In almost all the legends about dragon slayers, the heroes were giants.

"Take that with a grain of salt, Lady Yui! If I really was descended from the giants, I'd be bragging about it to everyone! I'm just an ordinary human, common as dirt."

"Hee-hee, if you say so... Well, Lady Yui? Would you like to try swimming now?" Luroo asked me.

It seemed that Senri was often teased about being part giant. She always denied it, but her superhuman strength got people thinking.

The merfolk were famous for their swimming ability.

Luroo and I entered the hot spring. She held my hand, leading me deeper in...and then, in a puff of magic, she transformed.

Her blue scales sparkled. Her hair, which was also blue, intensified in color until it glistened...and then somehow grew twice as long.

Her scales were beautiful, like little gemstones. They grew along her hairline and her forehead, covering her neck, arms, and the backs of her hands. Mermaids apparently don't have scales on their torsos—that's something I learned from the Encyclopedia of Races.

Most merfolk were female, with very few males. Mermaids could have children with land-dwellers, too, but while their daughters were always born as mermaids, their sons were usually of the same race as their father.

Merfolk could move their hair freely underwater, and while they were submerged, there was nothing their hair wouldn't cut. It made for a formidable weapon.

"You're so pretty..."

"Tee-hee. Thank you."

I didn't say that just as a pleasantry. The dim cave was now illuminated by the blue light of Luroo's magic, the water reacting to it. She was a lot like a fairy, in my eyes.

Luroo pulled me by the hand, and with her help, I swam—for the first time since my rebirth. Since I was used to swimming, I calmly let the water carry me.

Plus, I could breathe underwater. I discovered this back when the Nuir maids "bathed" me. Every four days, they would throw me into the bath and hold me underwater to get me clean so that I wouldn't sully the garments I was sewing. One of my fairy familiars—the one with bunny ears, who I called Moontide Fairy—didn't have legs under her dress, but a fish tail. She seemed to have dual affinities—moon and water—and it was thanks to her that I could breathe underwater. Before I realized that, I used to hold my breath until it hurt. Baths were less traumatic once I found out I could just breathe as normal.

"You seem quite comfortable with swimming, Lady Yui," Luroo said to me.

Moving House

"I can...breathe...underwater."

"Some people with water fairies still can't swim. They sink like stones!"

Luroo pulled me under. What I saw there took my breath away.

Wow—incredible. So many water fairies!

At the base of the crystal pillar rising out of the bottom of the hot spring, fairies were being born one after another.

While I was busy being mesmerized by the sights, Luroo pulled me down to the foot of the underwater pillar where fairies were being born. I saw writing carved into the pillar—PORTAL 15: LABYRINTH HOT SPRING. The pillar was made of crystal, and the inscription was underwater, so it was only visible once we got close to it. But the strangest thing of all was that it was in Japanese.

Water fairies kept popping into existence around me...only for half of them to merrily disappear.

Their magic must be strong...and maybe unstable, too? Or rather...is there a warp portal here? No way—that's video game logic...

I rubbed my temples.

Come to think of it, this is a fantasy world...

"What's the matter? Is the fairies' magic too strong for you?"

"Huh?! I can...hear you?"

We were underwater, but I could hear Luroo's voice perfectly well. My own voice sounded normal, too!

Luroo giggled at my confused expression.

"So you knew you could breathe underwater, but not that you could speak, too?"

"I've never...tried..."

Is this for real? Wow—it's amazing what fairies can do! Maybe the water vibrates with sound just like the air?

"There are lots of water fairies around us, aren't there?"

"Can you...sense them?"

"Yes. Like I said, I'm very attuned to water fairies."

I swam closer to the crystal pillar.

"It's just like the crystal at the boundary. It appears to be man-made."

"Magic is...welling up...from the base."

"Yes. It's responding to your own magic."

Really?

"I've visited this hot spring before, but it's never been like this."

"Ah."

Someone would've probably mentioned it if it was a regular occurrence.

I stepped onto the crystal's pedestal. A magic orb and a magic tablet appeared in front of me.

"Whoa!" I cried. "A map?"

"The magic here is materializing. It happens sometimes in labyrinths."

Luroo reached to touch the orb, but her hand went straight through it. I saw that the tablet had numbers one to twenty written on it, with *Labyrinth Hot Spring* written next to number fifteen. I poked it with my finger to see what would happen. My finger didn't go through the tablet—I touched it just like any real, physical object. The orb spun around and a point on it lit up. On closer inspection, it looked like a globe.

"So you *can* touch it."

"Oh..."

The area displayed on the globe was this continent. I saw the Menesmetlo

region, and one spot in the city was marked with a glowing dot of water magic. The tablet and the globe must have been linked somehow, and the globe was showing me the location of the portal.

"The labyrinth hot spring..."

I found the Royal Palace on the globe. There was a dot of golden magic on it. I thought about Aria. There were only two glowing dots in this country, but I counted as many as twenty-one on the globe. One more than the numbers on the tablet.

One of the glowing dots was much bigger than the others. It was shaped like a diamond, and it was located on another continent. When I touched it, text appeared on the top part of the tablet, which had been blank before. The numbers one through twenty remained unlit.

The text read *Portal 0: Seat of God*.

"I've never seen writing like this," said Luroo.

Of course not. It's in Japanese.

"It says...'Seat...of God,'" I told her.

Suddenly, I heard ringing in my head.

"New transmigrated person detected. Confirm warp to the Seat of God?"

Just as this electronic-sounding voice spoke to me, a sort of link formed in my mind.

What's going on?

I felt a warm, tingling sensation deep in my brow. It was strange, but not unpleasant. Luroo seemed oblivious to what had happened to me.

"The legendary Seat of God?! Isn't that located on that mythical continent?!"

She leaned closer to the globe, brimming with curiosity...but something pushed her away.

"My, what's this? A magical force field...?"

"A voice asked me...if I want to warp there. Did you...hear it?"

"...Hm? No, I didn't hear any voices. H-hold on. Lady Yui, please come this way."

I took Luroo's hand and let her lead me away from the crystal pillar. The tablet and the orb disappeared along with the sensation of a link in my head.

"Lady Yui, warp portals are not unusual in labyrinths. At least, portals that warp to the inner parts of the labyrinth. But this..."

"It's similar?"

"No, it's not. The Seat of God... That's where creation takes place..." Luroo gazed into the distance, thinking. "Lady Yui, may I ask you to hold off on trying to warp there? I suspect you may be the only person who can use that portal. And going to the Seat of God might have very serious consequences."

"Because it's legendary? On a mythical continent?"

"Because gods dwell there. And people and fairies who lay their eyes on gods become vastly more powerful."

I glanced at the spider sitting on my shoulder. It had become a creature similar to a fairy, which might eventually evolve into a divine beast.

"Would it...work on my spider, too?"

"Yes, I think so. It might instantly evolve into a divine beast."

Oh no! Aria said she'd die when one of her clones became a divine beast. So that would kill her! And if she died, it might become impossible to trigger the battle with the former queen's curse. There'd be no way to save the Realm Weaveguardian!

"Lady Yui, let's leave the hot spring. Please go on ahead. I'd like to take another look at the crystal."

Moving House

* * *

I broke through the surface with a splash, coughing up water as if I'd barely escaped drowning, even though I was perfectly fine.

"L-Lady Yui! Are you all right?!"

Alarmed, Stolle rushed to pat my back and lift me out of the water.

"What happened? Didn't your water fairy protect you?"

"I-it's…just a…bad habit…"

I didn't feel as if there was water in my lungs, or even as if I'd gulped down lots of water while swimming. Moontide Fairy somehow made it so that any water in my lungs immediately turned into air. But this change didn't apply to the water in my mouth at the moment I came back up, which sent me into a coughing fit that looked very painful. I didn't have any control over it.

At the Nuir residence, I had to convincingly act as if I'd nearly drowned after each of the "baths," which was why my fairy let some water remain in my mouth.

"At my home…the maids…liked to bully me…"

Snap! Senri crushed the water bucket she was holding.

"…My apologies. I clutched it too hard."

"Are you saying this coughing is a habit you acquired then?" Stolle asked.

I nodded.

"I was afraid…someone at my house…was hurting fairies. So I couldn't let them…find out about…the fairies protecting me."

"I understand. But you should tell your fairy that there's no longer any need to make it look as if you'd been drowning," Endelia told me with a heartfelt smile, stroking my back.

I felt a little embarrassed.

"But where is Luroo?"

"Ah! At the bottom of the spring…there's a portal!"

Just as I turned around, Luroo emerged from the hot spring. She absorbed her magic back into her body, shook herself dry, and reverted to her human form. Her usual kindly smile was gone, replaced by a very serious expression.

CHAPTER 3

Portal

We left the hot spring. I sipped delicately floral-scented water while the others talked.

"It's a mythic artifact?"

"Without doubt, since the portal leads to the Seat of God," Luroo said, and everyone gasped.

"A mythic artifact…?"

That's what items believed to be crafted by gods were called. The most famous of them was the Sword of Judgment used for selecting the emperor of a now lost continent—the demons' magical sword. Currently, the demon nation occupied a rather inhospitable region north of Lomestometlo Kingdom. The magically gifted demon race had reflected on their past mistakes and adopted a pacifistic philosophy.

Most of the other mythic artifacts chose their own masters. Crafted by the gods, they possessed unimaginable power, yet no wars were being waged over them among humans or demons. Fighting over artifacts that chose who they served was pointless.

It was only in the ancient past, when the world was unstable, that people tried allying themselves with the humans these mythic artifacts had chosen. A long streak of conflicts ended in the demon empire's continent being wiped off the map.

Who'd have thought we'd come across a mythic artifact at the bottom of a hot spring?

"As soon as Lady Yui came out of the water, the portal became invisible. I couldn't even get close to where it was. Some force was keeping me out."

"Only the worthy are allowed to approach it…," Endelia said quietly.

Mimachi was sitting despondently at Endelia's feet, her sight still blocked by Endelia's fairy.

"…I—I checked the hot spring to ensure it was safe," Mimachi said, "but I failed to sense the portal on the crystal's pedestal. S-some scout I am…"

"It's a mythic artifact, made by the gods. Don't blame yourself for not being able to detect it."

"It was truly unbelievable. Lady Yui was as calm as always, even as we entered the vortex of magical energy… How could that power be completely hidden from everyone except us? Even Endelia didn't notice anything. It makes me shudder!"

"What? A vortex of energy?"

Stolle's face gradually paled as Luroo continued relating what had happened.

"It was so strong—every second, dozens of fairies were being born or reabsorbed into the world."

"Hold on! Are you saying it was like a power vein?!" Mimachi practically screamed.

"And Endelia didn't pick up on it? That's insanely high-level masking!"

"Let's report this to His Highness. To anyone but the chosen, it's just

Portal

a regular hot spring. Luroo, did you collect water samples while the portal was visible and after it vanished?"

Luroo opened her hands, showing us what looked like marbles.

"When the energy vortex was active, I was only able to collect ones this size."

"Wait!" cried Mimachi. "Ms. Water-Is-My-Element! I can't sense any power from these things!"

"There is a reason I couldn't carry anything bigger than these droplets… Maybe you'll all feel their power when Lady Yui holds one."

The moment Luroo passed one of the marble-like drops to me, everyone except Luroo and Senri almost buckled, as if under heavy weight. They gasped, fighting to withstand this pressure. Meanwhile, I was completely unaffected. Luroo had been feeling the droplets' energy the whole time, so there was no change in her, either. But the strangest thing of all was…

Senri was literally dripping with cold sweat.

Everyone began staring at her. She raised her hand shakily.

"I'm very sorry. While Lady Yui and Luroo were in the hot spring, I heard a strange voice. It asked for warp confirmation…"

My eyes widened in shock.

"Huh? You…heard it, too?"

I tried asking her if she'd transmigrated from another world, but my voice disappeared midway:

"Did you also   ?"

Whoa, what just happened?!

"Lady Yui?! You're a   too?! Huh?!"

We both covered our mouths in shock. I heard the electronic voice from earlier speak directly to my brain again.

*   *   *

"Forbidden words detected."

Somehow, the voice sounded amused.

A few seconds later, I realized that perhaps Senri and I weren't thinking about the same thing after all.

"What I said was forbidden? Well, I should've guessed! But I swear, I'm an ordinary human! I just happen to be unusually strong! It would be less far-fetched to say I've got some giantess blood in me!"

Senri lay down on the floor and slammed her fists against it loudly. The ground shook like in an earthquake.

Stolle quickly picked me up in her arms. The floor cracked open, with the fissure stretching from one wall to another. It began to close as we watched.

The floor is repairing itself?

"This cave is part of the labyrinth. Any damage to it is repaired automatically. The bigger the damage, the faster it's fixed. Senri hit the floor with more power than Mimachi crashed into the wall earlier," Endelia explained.

"I didn't just crash into the wall. Stolle threw me into it!"

"Lady Yui, Senri. Can you tell us what makes you eligible to interact with the portal?" Endelia continued, ignoring Mimachi's interjection.

"My grandfather and my grandmother both ⸺⸺⸺⸺⸺ — Ugh, I'm trying to say it, but my lips won't even move!"

"   ." I tried to say in Japanese that I'd transmigrated from Japan, but my lips didn't move either.

Hmm… The talk about the power vein reminded me of what Aria told me about falling into an energy stream of some sort and meeting the gods. There was another portal in the Royal Palace, according to that globe. Aria said her mother used to be the final boss in the palace labyrinth…

"Is there a portal to Aria?"

* * *

"Warp to Ariadne, the Gatekeeper with third-degree authorization?"

My spider started glowing.

"No! Don't!"

I pressed my spider to my chest in a tight embrace, and the glow faded away. That was close!

"Lady Yui? Are all right?!"

"You can use the warp portal even when you're away from it…?"

Luroo cocked her head at me, puzzled. She then looked over at Senri.

"Did you hear a voice, too, Senri?"

"Ugh, who are you?! What does 'third-degree authorization' mean? Who's this 'Gatekeeper'?"

"I am the Gatekeeper, Guide. Third-degree authorization refers to those who have transmigrated to this world. You, Senri, possess second-degree authorization due to   . Information about degrees of authorization is restricted. Gatekeepers are beings who oversee portals and any information related to them."

"But…Aria didn't tell me about…portals?"

I looked at my spider, who returned my questioning gaze.

"Ariadne's Gatekeeper privileges are currently sealed. She does not have permission to share portal information."

"Sealed? By who…?"

"The gods and Gatekeeper Ariadne herself."

* * *

"Ah… Was she…just a provisional Gatekeeper?"

Aria wanted to be reborn as a human, so I doubt she'd take on such a burdensome role.

Ding-ding-ding! ♪

I heard a chime in my head, like a sound played in quiz shows when a contestant got the answer right.

"Yes. I am the official Gatekeeper."

The voice sounded a little proud.
"Feeling self-important, huh…"
Senri seemed fed-up.
"Are you okay, Senri?"
"Oh, Lady Yui…"
Still sitting on the cave floor, she looked up at me, her eyes brimming with tears.
"I have third-degree authorization…and you have second-degree?" I asked.
Someone other than a reincarnate, who could use portals… What did Aria say about the reason why people were reborn in this different world?

Transmigrated as…divine vessels? Or…their relatives?

"Senri, do you speak Japanese?" I asked her in Japanese.
"Oh! You speak the language of my grandparents' homeland?! I managed to learn some words, but I can't really speak it."
"So your grandparents   ?"

Portal

Suddenly, a shadow stretched from under my feet to my neck.

"Lady Yui!"

"Lady Yui?!"

Nobody could do anything to stop it.

There was the *clink* of a lock snapping into place followed by a metallic rattling. I now had a metal collar around my neck, with a chain that disappeared in my shadow. I was very aware that it was there, but I couldn't touch or move it, so it must have been made from pure magic. My very confused-looking dark fairy was sitting on the floor after getting kicked out of my shadow.

"Guide! What have you done to Lady Yui?!"

"A person with third-degree authorization has inferred the meaning of the degrees of authorization. I had to take emergency measures."

I guess...that's a bad thing?

But these portals were made by gods. It's not that hard to figure out who these authorized people are.

The first degree of authorization must've referred to people who'd been reborn as divine vessels, the second degree to their relatives, and the third degree to the ordinary reborn like me.

"Hold on! What 'emergency measures'? What does that have to do with Lady Yui?!"

Senri had turned white as a sheet. Seeing her so shaken made me realize that nobody was supposed to be able to just work out the authorization rules by themselves.

"Is this...to protect you, Senri?"

"Lady Yui?! How did you...?"

"Ah, I see…!" said Mimachi. "Lady Yui tried to say something naughty out loud, hmm?"

Endelia had released her, and she was now inspecting the chain dangling from the collar to my shadow. She got down on her hands and knees, peering at it closely.

"This isn't magic. Looks to me like some divine power."

"You must be right, if it forced the dark fairy out of Lady Yui's shadow."

"But how can we free her?!"

Everyone had gone pale, even Mimachi. Her tone was as usual, but her facial expression was strained.

"…"

"It's m-m-my fault, isn't it…?"

Senri looked completely crushed, as if she was the one chained up and being weighted down.

"No, Senri… It's not…your fault," I said as I quietly moved my feet.

"Wow!"

My legs moved as if I was walking, but I hadn't moved an inch. Wasn't there a dance move like that in my old world? Not that I knew how to do it. I found it a bit funny. I tried waving my hand and saw that my shadow didn't move.

"It looks like Lady Yui's shadow has been bound to the labyrinth," said Mimachi. "The labyrinth's expansion and contraction effect is applied to her shadow."

I remembered the labyrinth Aria had spawned.

"You mean I…can't leave?"

"I doubt it, even if someone carried you… And if someone tried to move you away from your shadow by force, that collar might choke you."

My hand instinctively went to my neck.

"If that's…how it is…"

Portal

I reached out toward Moontide Fairy with a magic string, which she chomped down on. I asked her to dehumidify our immediate surroundings.

"Let's…get changed."

I didn't want to still be in my bathing suit when Argit came down here to talk to me.

"! I'll go and report everything that happened to Sir Argit!" Luroo offered.

"I'll stay by Lady Yui's side to protect her."

"Nuh-uh, Stolle! You've got to stuff yourself back into your armor. You'd hate Sir Argit to see you like this, right?"

Mimachi's teasing gave Stolle pause.

"Well, Stolle needs to get her armor, since it's too cumbersome for someone else to bring all the pieces for her in one trip," said Endelia. "I think it's best if Senri stays here for now. I'll fetch clothes for Lady Yui, Senri, and Mimachi."

Endelia took Stolle's hand and tugged, urging her to come with her. Senri's raised hand dropped limply to her side as Endelia preempted her before she could say she'd get Stolle's armor.

"Senri, please stay with Lady Yui and keep an eye on Mimachi, so that she won't do anything indecent."

"Come on now, even I'm not so without morals to take advantage of Lady Yui in this situation, honest!"

We put our clothes back on, and everyone sat around me. I carefully perched myself atop one of the cushions, making sure my feet were still in contact with my pinned shadow. Mimachi used her magic powers to create a low table out of rock. While she was doing that, she discovered that the area where my shadow had been pinned blocked magic—which we'd suspected already, given that even my dark fairy was repelled from it. While fairies were banned from my shadow, people could walk over it—except Stolle in her fairy armor.

Argit arrived in a hurry. His eyes narrowed when he sensed the heavy force around me, and when he saw the collar around my neck, he gasped in terror.

"Is it hurting you?"

"No, I'm fine."

After checking that it was safe for other people to enter my shadow, before anyone could stop him, Argit sat down on the floor beside me. He pulled me into an embrace, so that I could lean back against his chest.

I allowed myself to melt into that embrace, comforted by the warmth of Argit's body. I wasn't too worried about this predicament, since the people with divine powers in this world were my fellow Japanese and they were Senri's grandparents, but it seemed that I had unconsciously tensed up.

A light meal and drink had been placed on the table in front of me, with balls of yarn and knitting needles in a wicker basket next to it.

"Lady Yui, please eat first," Endelia said to me with a smile, stopping me from reaching for the basket.

I was given a slice of savory pie, with a thin layer of cream on the bottom, onions and bacon, tomato sauce, and the most perfectly poached egg on top. I was told that the egg had been poached in a dedicated spot of this hot spring where the water was warmest. I was willing to bet that this place was created by a Japanese person. Maybe Senri's grandparents.

The cream turned out to be some kind of potato mash. It was sweet, reminding me of Asian sweet potatoes. It went great with the onions, bacon, and the sweet-and-sour tomato sauce. The crispy pie crust was the finishing touch.

For everyone else, this would be a snack, but for me, this one slice was a full meal. And I've made considerable progress with how much I can eat. I used to be unable to finish even half of a pie like this.

I ate while reclining against Argit as he was briefed about the events before and after our discovery of the portal. He rubbed his temples with one hand.

Senri was the only one aside from me who could hear Guide's voice, so she had to fill in the last details. With her eyes unfocused as if she was trying to dissociate, she relayed what had happened.

"Have you asked this Guide about conditions for Yui's release?"

A look of surprise crossed Senri's face.

"Guide!" she quickly shouted. "Can you please tell me what needs to be done for you to release Lady Yui?!"

"...I ask for your patience while I conduct an analysis to determine what constraints must be applied to her. She must remain as is in order to prevent interaction with Ariadne."

"Constraints?!"

"An analysis...to determine constraints...?"

Ah, so he was checking to see if I have any abilities that would harm Senri? I didn't think I had any, but even if I did, I guess he'd do something to make sure I wouldn't use them against her.

"What's this about constraining Lady Yui?!"

Everyone seemed terrified.

I was later told that, based on the chain and collar around my neck, they thought this entity was going to enslave me. Meanwhile, I was the least bothered of everyone there.

Portal

* * *

"If a person with second- or third-degree authorization travels to the Seat of God to formally request an appraisal, I will also be able to release Yui."

"I'll go! I'll go to this Seat of God, if that's what's needed to set Lady Yui free!"

As soon as she'd said it, Senri glowed faintly, and vanished.

"No, Senri, wait!"

I raised my hand to stop her, but it was too late. She said she'd go, and she was teleported without a moment's delay. Just like when I was making the pact with my spider, words had immediate consequences.

"Senri… You should've asked first…what this appraisal meant…"

I lowered my hand slowly.

"You wish to know what the appraisal entails? Your resolve and determination will be tested, and you will be evaluated to see whether power might blind you."

"But isn't this…analysis you spoke about something like that, too? When will that be finished? And if the results are good, will I be free?"

"Affirmative. My analysis of your fairy guardians' abilities is complete, and the results do not raise concerns. Your release is already being processed and will take effect in five minutes."

"…It seems…I'll be released in five minutes," I told everyone.

Endelia sighed deeply.

"That Senri... Such a hot-headed girl. She never thinks before she acts."

Everyone besides me could only hear my half of the conversation with Guide, but it was enough for them to understand that Senri went to the Seat of God for nothing.

"I hope she won't get in trouble by trying to argue with the gods..."

Argit's remark was met with worried gasps, but I had the impression that nobody fully realized the weight of what was happening—Senri had casually travelled to some unknown place. She'd probably be fine, though. If I was right about her grandparents, then she was something like a grandchild to a god of this world, and grandparents are very forgiving to their grandchildren, as long as their mischief is nothing outrageous.

◆

Since I had so little energy, I fell asleep as usual just five minutes after my post-bath meal. That habit was so reliable you could set your clock by it. I woke up in bed, in a very pretty room. I looked out the window. The sky was overcast, but it was definitely morning already. I brought my hand to my neck to check if the collar was gone—it was—and then I got out of bed. I was a little astonished that I'd managed to fall asleep while I was still being restrained, unable to wait the few minutes for my release.

"Good morning, Lady Yui! ♪"

"Good...morning..."

Mimachi suddenly materialized next to my bed. She'd always appear when I woke up, so I was used to it by then. I washed my face in the washbowl she'd brought me, and she gently dried me off with a towel. That done, she gave me a fresh change of clothes. As soon as I took them from her, Mimachi's eyes clouded over. My dark fairy, Purple Prince, was sitting on

her shoulder, facing away from her. If there was nobody else around, he'd always come out and block Mimachi's sight to make sure she'd behave while I was changing.

"Grr... You give me no chance..."

It occurred to me that Purple Prince was unusual in that he'd interact with people and objects to help me without me giving him any magic, like when he cut blessed threads for me.

After I got dressed, Mimachi carefully combed my hair. She'd put a few drops of wonderfully scented oil on the comb.

"Did Senri...come back yet?"

"Yes, she did!"

I guessed from Mimachi's cheery tone that Senri was fine. What a relief. She was a god's grandchild, so she was probably sent right back without any problems.

"But, oh boy, what a sight she is now!"

"?"

"You'd better see for yourself." Mimachi snorted with laughter. "And by the way, since you're safe, the others have gone out."

"Others...?"

"Sir Argit and Endelia are meeting someone at the labyrinth."

"Oh?"

"Turns out, one of the adventurers who helped Sir Argit obtain his ice sword from another labyrinth is currently a member of the Labyrinth Guild and supposedly has a wind fairy. His Highness and Endelia are going to check if that's true." Mimachi looked out the window. "They're kind of in a hurry to find the right person. Once it snows, the city will become inaccessible."

◆

"Goodness..."

I couldn't help commenting, somewhat in shock.

Senri was sitting with her head down on the dining room table, and a strange male figure was hovering around her shoulders. He was pretty much naked, and blue from head to foot. He had a piece of cloth wrapped around his loins and was wearing sandals, but no other clothing. Something that looked like vines twisted around his thighs.

Glittering gem-like scales, similar to Luroo's mermaid scales, reached from his legs up to the sides of his abdomen. His ears were shaped like fish fins, but behind them were horns, like the kinds on Asian dragons. The horns were blue, and they, too, sparkled like jewels. His hair floated in the air, fading away into it.

"...A fairy?" I said.

He vaguely reminded me of Purple Prince.

"This fella's a half fairy. My dragonkin father unsealed power which I had unconsciously locked away, being unable to control it, to create him as my guardian. To think my father, the most timid, introverted member of my family, would do such a thing!"

I could see now why Senri said it'd be more believable about her being descended from giants.

The half fairy was watching her with amusement. Unlike normal fairies, he had a physical body, even though he was floating in the air. If there was anything I could compare him to, it was the thread spun by Aria—magic made material.

"Dragonkin..."

Right, so... As far as I remembered, the dragonkin were a very proud race, to the point of haughtiness. They possessed tremendous power, too. Since they never interbred with other races, and were very rare to begin with, they were said to have died out...but apparently, that information was incorrect.

The dragonkin were the most elusive of the mythical races.

"Wow…"

I was speechless. Senri's dad was a dragonkin, so it must have been her mom who descended from the gods. What a family! I glanced over at Mimachi, who didn't seem particularly impressed, so maybe it was only me who was so amazed by all of this.

"Well, my grandparents are   , so my dad never had much say in the house," Senri mumbled, covering her face with her hands. "Anyway, what bothers me the most is that this guy won't wear anything besides a loincloth!"

The half fairy leaning over Senri had a beautiful physique, with a six-pack and curves from his waist to his thighs that looked too sexy on a man.

"He has a physical body, but you can't make him wear anything he doesn't like."

"If only your half fairy was a woman, she'd be a feast for the eyes." Mimachi tutted with a momentarily lecherous gaze.

Senri seemed really exhausted by her new inseparable familiar.

"Lady Yui, if I may ask you for only one thing—please make him some clothes!" Senri pleaded, almost in tears.

I asked for more details about this half fairy and was told that gods made him by taking powers that Senri couldn't control and mixing that with seawater.

He had a gorgeous male figure—and he was nearly nude. Plus, he had a physical form, so anyone could see him, or touch him.

"You're…Senri's bodyguard?"

The half fairy smiled at me and nodded.

"Lady Yui, please make clothes for him…!"

"I…don't think I can."

"Yeah...," Mimachi agreed. "Lady Yui's blesswoven garments would only weaken his power."

"No, I think he's...wary of me."

I was one hundred percent certain he'd decline anything I made for him. I pointed to myself, cocking my head, but before the half fairy had the chance to respond, I heard a loud noise. Senri had banged her head on the table in frustration.

"Oh, look! The table isn't broken!"

Mimachi clapped. While normally tables wouldn't break just from someone slamming their head against them, in Senri's case, it was an achievement to leave it undamaged. I reflexively clapped too, and it was only then that I realized the room felt strangely empty.

"Is Stolle...not here either...?"

"She went to get a carriage."

"Why?"

"We can't use Sir Argit's carriage, so we need another."

Mimachi began to recount what had happened while I was asleep.

"A short while after you passed out, your shadow got unpinned. At first, we weren't sure what this Guide person decided to do with you, but when it seemed okay to take you away from the hot spring, we carried you to your room and put you in bed. I then went to get pills which temporarily let people without water fairies breathe underwater, and when I came back, Senri had returned, too."

Without lifting her head off the table, Senri raised her hand.

"I can't tell you the details, because I promised the gods to keep it secret, but I met my grandparents."

"Your grandparents..."

"Um... Lady Yui, I believe you've guessed that my grandparents have a special connection with the gods, and that's why they can use the portals. The gods contacted them, and they came to see me... I got told off for being too impulsive, and for not controlling my power well enough."

I could see why—Senri was acting madder than a box of cats when she teleported to the Seat of God.

"Guide reported to the gods that Lady Yui has no battle skills or other attack abilities, but she has the king of dark fairies as her familiar, so the gods decided to make Kairi for me, out of my own power, and assign him as my guardian just in case."

Hold on... The half fairy has a name? Kairi, as in the kanji for "sea" and "hometown"? Then maybe Senri's name is Japanese too, written with kanji for "thousand" and "hometown"? That's just a guess, though; there are lots of different ways to write "ri" in Japanese.

My mind went to the spelling of names, since the other shocking bit of information was a bit too much.

My dark fairy...was the king of his kind?

"This is...the king of dark fairies?"

He was hovering near my shoulder. I fished him out of the air with my hands and held him in front of my face. He struck a pose, puffing out his chest and smiling smugly. It was very cute.

I thought nobody except me could see him, but Kairi chuckled at Purple Prince's posing.

"Whaaat?! He can make sounds?!"

"Uh, that kind of startled me, too, but more importantly... Lady Yui's dark fairy is a fairy king?"

Well, I hadn't seen any male fairies besides him, and he was dressed like

a prince. He could also interact with real objects without being given magic, so I knew he was special... Wait, he wasn't the only one...

"Um... You said...the gods made Kairi for you? Did the water fairies not have a king before him?"

"He's not the king of water fairies, but of sea fairies."

"Wait, I've never heard of sea fairies before..."

"Yes, that's because there hadn't been any until now."

"Huh?! And you didn't think to tell me that a whole new type of fairies has just been created?!"

Mimachi pounded the table with her fists. That finally made Senri sit upright in her chair.

"I couldn't. The gods forbade me. I'm allowed to tell Lady Yui about the gods' 'gift' to me, though, so that she'd know my familiar can match her dark fairy king."

Senri tried to say more, but her mouth shut unnaturally, as if not by her own volition.

"Ah, I see. You can only talk about that in Lady Yui's presence, and some of that information is for Lady Yui's ears only, huh?" Mimachi asked Senri.

"...That's it, yes."

"And is Stolle getting a carriage...because you can't stay near me anymore, Senri?"

The thought of her leaving made me so sad. I felt my chest tighten painfully. I noticed I was clutching my skirt in my fists.

Senri entered Rodin's service right after me. She chose the same days off as me to keep me company and would often help me carry my shopping. She was as close to me as Linne. When I got engaged to Argit, she became my personal maid... But would she be leaving me now?

"Huh? No, no, no! It's because of the portal. I've been asked to help restore the portal at the Royal Palace!"

"You'll be restoring the portal...?"

That was totally unexpected. My tears stopped at once. The portal at the palace was the one Aria was in charge of.

"Your ancestor's spider somehow got involved during that portal's creation. My family moved to this country to help release her, and in—install? Install Guide in her place." Senri sighed. "But when my grandparents came to this country at the gods' request, Lady Yui's grandfather had just become the new head of the Nuir household. The other spiders and their owners had been...dealt with. My grandparents couldn't awaken the original spider, because her spirit was at risk of being extinguished."

...That was a wild story. Why did my family suddenly turn into villains when my grandfather took charge? Before him, we seemed to enjoy a good reputation, didn't we?

"And so, my grandparents weren't able to carry out their task. As their descendant, it falls to me to restore the portal."

"Oh, Lady Yui, you don't need to trouble yourself to go there!" Mimachi insisted. "That area is, like, supervised by another Guide, apparently? Anyway, you can just stay here while Senri takes care of the portal!"

That seemed reasonable.

"You didn't know about any of this...until now?" I asked Senri.

"My parents did, but I didn't. Everybody was sure that unless a seamstress able to properly blessweave was born within my parents' lifetime, the spirit of your ancestor's spider wouldn't survive. So, in that respect, the gods are grateful to you."

It chilled me to the bone to think Aria was so close to being erased from existence. I gently stroked my spider's head.

"I need to go and get the tools for installing Guide from my parents

Portal

first, and then I'll head to the royal palace. Although my parents might want to come along, too."

"If we can get the portal restored, it'll make it much easier to regularly deliver healing gloves made by Lady Yui, among other things."

"? How so?"

"While only a select few are allowed to travel to the Seat of God, and some other destinations are too dangerous, generally up to six people with authorization can use the portals to teleport together."

Oh, that sounded useful. Instant travel between the royal palace and this residence! With the portal open, I could easily get the king and Hania to try on the battle garments I was making them to see if any alterations were needed. And let's not forget I was going to make them wedding outfits, as well!

"Our king's also in the battle party, despite the danger," said Mimachi. "If Senri can get the portal to work again, His Majesty will be able to sneakily come over to the labyrinth for battle practice!"

"By the way, both me and Kairi have been forbidden from taking part in the battle."

"It's okay, Senri. Nobody was expecting you to join the team anyway. You're monstrously strong, but too klutzy for it to be of much use."

Mimachi chuckled. Senri hung her head, but I noticed a happy little smile playing on her lips.

Senri had told me that she became a maid precisely because she had zero talent for combat. When she was a little girl, an aspiring adventurer she knew pestered her to come along to a battle, since she was insanely strong—except that when it turned out she was hopeless at fighting, her acquaintance got really mad at her. That episode was quite traumatic for Senri, and ever since, she had gotten even worse at controlling her power.

"My parents told me that if I don't want to put my power to use, I need to learn to contain it... But the gods found a different solution."

"The gods...did you a favor?"

"Um... Y-yes, I think it was kind of them. I'm grateful to Kairi, too. If only it weren't for his shameless appearance!"

Hmm. He did exist in the material realm, but wouldn't his clothes represent his magic power, like in other fairies?

"Senri...can you ask him if...he'd allow me to make him clothes out of magic...instead of normal cloth?"

If he'd been born with that loincloth he was wearing, it must've been part of his magical power.

"Huh?"

"He's a half fairy, but...fairy clothes are made of...magical power. Could you ask Kairi if he'd wear...garments made of magic?"

Right away, Mimachi took writing tools and a bunch of paper out of her bag. I'd been sketching designs for Argit in my spare time when we were staying at inns. I could adapt some of those designs for Kairi—the color palettes and styles would suit him just as well. He had dragon horns, though, and that sexy body. I thought about basing his garments on clothing traditionally worn by women, for a more androgynous look. A Chinese dress, or maybe an *áo dài*!

I laid out a fresh sheet of paper. I was going to design a matching outfit for Senri as well.

"Wait, Lady Yui! Why are you sketching clothes for me?"

"It may make...your fairy happy...to have matching outfits!"

I was hoping that this would stoke Kairi's enthusiasm for crafting garments out of magic. I looked up from my sketches and saw that he was finally showing interest in the designs, craning his neck to see them over Senri's shoulder.

"Seems like it'll work!"

"What? Oh, but..."

Senri followed my gaze to Kairi and began despairing again.

"No, wait. Me and Kairi, in matching outfits? You want to dress *me* in the same style as this hunk?!"

"Hmm, you've got a point. Even for a girl, it's hard to rival his beauty, eh? Well, good luck! ★"

"Don't worry, Senri! I'll come up with…a design to suit you!"

I was planning to make Kairi's outfit revealing and alluring, but for Senri, I'd make a neat and proper one. She'd surely agree to matching styles then! Wouldn't she? Well, fingers crossed…

Designing flamboyant clothes for Kairi and a matching but modest outfit for Senri took me the whole morning.

Come noon, Stolle returned together with Gogol. They rode in a lavish carriage quite different from Argit's, with embellishments that made it clear it belonged to a noble. I supposed Stolle brought it from her own house. Meanwhile, Argit's carriage was being looked after at Stolle's parents' residence.

Mimachi and I were in the living room when the others arrived. We went out front to greet them.

I was under the impression that it was only Mimachi, Senri, and myself in the house, but it turned out Mijit was in the kitchen all along. He was the cook, so he had to prepare lunch.

By the way, I did eat my breakfast before getting started with sewing clothes for Senri. It was a Japanese-style breakfast; Mijit had noticed I liked that kind of cuisine. There was salmon (or some other salmon-like fish?), a rice ball, miso soup, and pickled daikon radishes.

The porch on the first floor led to the living room, with the kitchen at the back. I called it the first floor, but you had to climb a small staircase from the porch to reach it. Behind the kitchen was the pantry, and a larder as cold as a fridge.

Stolle and Gogol seemed relieved when they saw me. Stolle was in her full-body armor as usual, but I could tell how she was feeling.

"We've just made it back."

"Lady Yui, it's good to see you. How do you feel?"

Stolle knelt before me on one knee, took my hand, and gazed at my face.

"I feel fine."

"I must apologize to you, Lady Yui. You haven't even had the time to settle in yet, but already Senri and I must leave you to travel to the royal palace."

"And I'll be leaving, too. You can't ride without your coachman!"

I couldn't see it, but I guessed that Stolle shot Gogol a chilling stare. He flinched in terror.

"Mr. Gogol, the problem here is that there will be fewer women looking after Lady Yui, keeping her safe from Mimachi's follies!"

There were several men besides Argit who'd traveled here with us: Gogol the human coachman, Mijit the beastkin cook who had black ears and a tail like a dog's, a royal guard dispatched from the palace, and Argit's aide, who had gotten trapped inside Aria's labyrinth with us before (we hadn't been introduced yet, so I didn't know his name). They were pretty much strangers to me. The women in the group included Stolle, Endelia, Luroo, Senri, and the troublemaker Mimachi. Without Stolle and Senri, Endelia and Luroo would have their hands full keeping me safe.

Stolle clasped both my hands and touched her forehead to them, as if in prayer.

"Lady Yui, if I may ask you, please stay close to Endelia at all times."

"No need for that. I'm her bodyguard-maid!"

Stolle ignored Mimachi's protest.

"Are you leaving...now?" I asked.

Portal

"I'm afraid I must. Do you remember the hills we crossed on the way here? In a few days, heavy snowfall will make them almost impassable."

"Even hills get very dangerous once there's snow. Underestimate the danger, and you're dead," Mimachi added gravely.

"We have to leave in time to cross the hills before it snows."

Gogol gave a thin smile. Mijit handed him a basket, probably with lunch for them to eat on the way.

"I've been hired to take care of transportation for you, but I don't think I'll be coming back with the carriage," said Gogol. "You won't have a need for my services anymore once you get the portal open."

"Gogol isn't just a coachman. He has abilities enabling him to carry luggage on foot even through deep snow, as long as it's nothing too heavy. The original plan was to have him deliver gloves to the palace at regular intervals."

Oh, that sounded neat. But wait, he could carry luggage through snow all the way to the capital on foot?!

"Even Gogol would struggle to drive a carriage with passengers through deep snow."

"I was to deliver the gloves to Lord Rodin, who would then take them to the king. To be let into the palace, I'd need to be accompanied by a trusted noble of high rank like Lady Stolle here."

"I wouldn't count. Despite who my grandparents are, I'm just a commoner," Senri remarked, coming down from the second floor with a load of luggage.

She carried it as if it weighed next to nothing, so it seemed that she could still use her monstrous strength when she needed to.

"Apologies for having kept you waiting. Here's Gogol's bag, and here is Lady Stolle's."

"Thank you. I haven't even finished unpacking, which is just as well."

"Lady Yui, we must bid you farewell. We'll be back as soon as circumstances allow. When His Highness returns, please tell him we're on our way to the palace."

And so the three of them, along with Kairi, left the Menes family's secret retreat only a day after our arrival.

CHAPTER 4

Schnell

The man was lean and long-limbed, with deep fir-green hair past his shoulders. His eyes, the color of fresh spring leaves, were frozen in a permanent scowl. His overall strikingly handsome appearance led people to whisper that he might have some forest-folk blood in him.

From behind, he could be mistaken for a slender woman. The drunks who had made that mistake were lying on the floor of the guild tavern, beaten up.

He was wearing a coat in a shade of green so dark it was almost black, in a design accentuating his slim waistline, without restricting his movements. It had to be made to measure, and it made him stand out from the other adventurers. Endelia gasped in admiration, thinking that this well-dressed man could definitely be persuaded to help them if the reward was a garment made by Yui.

"It's him, isn't it?"

"Yes… It would seem he's been drinking all morning…"

Argit added under his breath that at least that meant he was quick to find. He could see the man's fairy—all green, almost transparent, in a very pretty dress. She was as tall as an adult man. When she noticed Argit looking, she whispered something into the adventurer's ear.

"Wazzat?" the man shouted in an unfriendly, menacing voice, turning around.

"It's been a while, hasn't it, Schnell?"

"...Huh. If it isn't Arjet," the man said warily.

"Arjet" was, of course, Argit's false name. Schnell looked Argit up and down with narrowed eyes. He then slammed his glass down on the counter so hard, it cracked with an unnerving noise.

"You lied to me, ya bastard! Where's yer clown outfit gone? The one you've supposedly gotta be wearin' all the time, on account of yer family's tradition!" Schnell was frowning deeply, speaking through his teeth. "This here top-notch blesswoven garment? Where'd ya get that from? Some ruined noble? How come it fits ya perfectly? I hate yer new playboy look. Go to hell."

"You seem to be in a sour mood today. What's gotten into you? I didn't take you for a morning drinker, either."

"Buzz off! What's it to you if I'm havin' a little celebration? Finally got that scoundrel who's been stickin' to me like a burr outta my hair!"

Schnell swung up his arm ungraciously, raising his cracked glass in a toast. If it hadn't been empty, he'd have splashed them.

"A rude newcomer has been following Schnell around until this morning, insisting that he join him," a passing guildmate of Schnell's explained to Argit.

"Ah, I see."

Argit and Endelia exchanged glances. Their timing couldn't have been worse.

"Why're ya still here? You want somethin'?"

"As it happens, we've come to invite you to our party."

Schnell

"*Invite* me?"

Schnell's voice was like an angry rumble from the depths of the earth. He glared at Argit.

"To save this particular fairy, we need either someone with a severance-type ability or a wind-property magic sword."

"Severance?"

Schnell glanced down at his beloved battle equipment hanging from his belt. He had a sturdy leather whip and a dungeon weapon—a paper fan for bludgeoning his opponents to death.

Weapons obtainable from dungeons, or labyrinths as they were usually called here, weren't all necessarily powerful. And then there were the gag weapons like Schnell's. A lucky adventurer might walk out of a labyrinth with a special, mighty weapon. But some of the prizes to be found there were entirely useless. Gag weapons were unusual in appearance, and while most of them had some use in battle, it was nothing to write home about.

Schnell's fan was a labyrinth weapon, but it was made of paper. It made a satisfying sound when used to slap somebody on the head while roasting them with an apt riposte. You'd have to try really hard to slap a person with it until they dropped unconscious, but when used against monsters, it was deadly. For some reason, gag weapons had been granted various unusual effects by the gods.

Which was all very well, but…

"My weapons don't have severance powers."

"I know this already."

"Right…"

Argit pressed his lips into a smile as Schnell eyed him warily.

"I can offer you a garment with the same level of blessings as the one I'm wearing as a reward. As should go without saying, it will be made to your order."

"Hold on!" Schnell left money on the bar counter and got up from his seat. "Which is it, then? You got a secret Nuir love child? Or did ya get lucky enough to find another spider-turned-divine-beast?" Schnell whispered into Argit's ear, putting an arm around his shoulders, sobered up by the offer he was evidently keen on.

"You're quite knowledgeable about blessweaving. But do you know what quality garments House Nuir has been producing as of late?"

"I shoulda mentioned the reason I came to this land. It was the Nuirs' blessweaving I was after."

Schnell invited Argit and Endelia to his room at the inn where he was staying, to show them something.

"I wanted to see for myself if the blessweaving was as precious as the rumors make it out to be, so I put in an order with the Nuirs as soon as I arrived in this country."

Schnell pulled out a shirt from one of his bags, which were lying in a pile on the floor.

"It cost me all the coin I'd saved up. I gave the Nuirs the finest shirt I made to be blesswoven…and this is what I got back from 'em."

The shirt was beautifully tailored, but jarring red and black threads stitched into the breast pocket in an ugly pattern completely ruined its otherwise impeccable appearance. It was clearly infused with magical power brutally ripped out of fairies, and the level of technique used was outrageously low.

"Goodness…"

"They even had the audacity to charge me an additional fee for the fairies' blessings sewn in."

"…Mr. Schnell, do correct me if I'm mistaken," Endelia began, "but the

front pocket threads seem to have gone through the back fabric as well? It's impossible to wear this shirt!"

"Either way, there's no force in hell that'd make me put on this filth!"

Schnell ground his teeth, pinching the shirt between his thumb and index finger with disgust.

"Blessings of the fairies? Lies! This is stolen fairy magic!"

"You can discern different types of magic, Schnell?"

"Tell ya what, the whole reason I teamed up with ya that time was because I saw ya were another victim of the very same atrocious seamster."

"The head of House Nuir…"

"Not anymore, right? He must've been replaced, by whoever made what yer wearin' now," Schnell said with a big grin, clapping his hands. "Serves that scumbag right! That's some good news. I should drink to this."

Schnell pulled out a locked chest from under his bed. He unlocked it and got a bottle of fine mead out of it. Argit waved his hands to stop him.

"We haven't come to watch you get drunk again, Schnell."

"Sorry, sorry. By the way, what's the deal with you, Arjet? Yer a noble, or ya wouldn't be dressed like this. Of high rank. Ya told me it's yer family's principle to wear only garments crafted by the Nuirs, though, and there's no putrid thread with stolen fairy magic in yer outfit. Quite the mystery."

Schnell set the unopened bottle of mead down on the table, looking at it longingly. Then he brought two chairs, putting them down in front of the bed. He sat on the bed and motioned for his guests to sit.

"You can see fairies, Arjet, am I right?"

"Yes."

"So can I. Gotta squint, though."

Schnell screwed up his eyes and looked straight at his fairy. His scowl was even more intimidating than his usual expression, but overall, his face softened.

"Ah, she's put on color, making herself easier to see."

"Put on color...?" asked Endelia.

Argit nodded.

"When I first met Schnell, I thought his was a high-level fairy of both fire and wind affinity, but the second time, she looked like an earth and wind fairy."

"So that's why ya pulled that shocked face back then."

"Later, I observed the non-wind affinity color gradually fade, until suddenly Schnell's fairy exchanged her magic with a nearby water fairy, taking on a blue hue. Right now, she's green."

"That's right. She can't hold onto other fairies' magic for long. Unlike the spider silk used in blessweavin', which preserves fairy magic indefinitely..." Schnell's voice was tinged with envy. "But even stolen magic must be sewn in fast, or it disappears."

Argit thought about how fairies would line up even before Yui began sewing, waiting to infuse her needlework with their magical power. They only did that for Yui, and the founder of House Nuir before her, apparently. The fairies didn't want to be near the other Nuirs' spiders.

Yui's father would feed stolen fairy magic to his spider to produce spider silk with fairies' blessings. Yet his work was slow—so slow that the magic would begin to dissipate before the threads could hold it fast. Maybe he didn't notice. Maybe he was oblivious to how him sewing the outrageously expensive garments all by himself actually lowered their value.

"Ah, this explains why there was so little magic left."

"Might it be that he refrained from using more of the stolen magic intentionally, so as not to draw the attention of the faysighted, who'd guess what he was guilty of?"

Argit considered Endelia's suggestion for a moment, but then shook his head. Yui's father was a short-sighted, greedy simpleton. He was so sure of himself, he brazenly asked for an additional fee for ruining Schnell's shirt. It was remarkable that he actually managed to preserve some of the stolen magic in the shirt, given the scale of his incompetence. How pleased he must have been at this achievement.

"No, that man is not smart enough to have thought of that. He was only the head of his household because of the spider pact. He was the only successor."

"Yes, you must be right."

"Tell me, Arjet, how did the person who made yer current outfit get their hands on a spider? I sense faymancers, those fairy magic thieves, by their repulsive aura. Likewise, threads containing stolen fairy magic feel disgustin' to me. But yer clothes feel clean. As if the fairies had offered their magic willingly. That's why my first thought was, it's gotta be a legendary family heirloom ya got off some desperate noble gone bankrupt."

Argit and Endelia felt the hair on the backs of their necks rise. It took Schnell just one look to correctly appraise the blessweaving in Argit's outfit as on par with the Nuir Founder's. Such keen perception often went hand in hand with outstanding ability. It wasn't uncommon for people with high-level fairy familiars to not benefit from their powers fully, as their own insensitivity to magic held their fairies back. But that wasn't the case here.

"Schnell, I suspect you're unable to wield your fairy's power. Is that right?"

"Huh?! I don't look like the type to be gettin' along with fairies, is that what yer sayin'?! Here I thought we were havin' a good chat, but outta the blue, ya insult me!"

Schnell glared furiously. Argit quickly shook his head.

"You misunderstand! You're clearly outstandingly gifted, so it's something of a mystery that your fairy's blessings seem to be beyond your reach."

"What are you talking about?"

"Master Argit, it might be worth introducing Mr. Schnell to Lady Yui, to seek her opinion," Endelia proposed.

Yui had been bringing about many changes, great and small. She unlocked the full power of Stolle's armor, awakened the Founder's spider, and even indirectly led to the unlocking of Senri's powers of divine heritage. Perhaps she could also solve the mystery of Schnell and his fairy, helping him access all of his fairy's abilities.

Argit gazed at the ceiling as he mulled over Endelia's suggestion. Finally, he nodded. While it might turn out that Yui couldn't do anything for Schnell, he'd thought about her too, so it might be worth a try.

"Who's this Lady Yui? And she called you Argit? Hmph, I had a feelin' Arjet was a fake name. Wait a sec, where'd I hear that name before…"

Schnell cocked his head, thinking, but he couldn't recall why the name sounded familiar. He sighed and adjusted himself on the bed, leaning in toward them.

"Lemme guess, Lady Yui is yer new seamstress? In that case, sure, I'll meet her! Take me to her! I can go now!"

"Schnell…?"

Argit and Endelia exchanged glances, confused by the shift in Schnell's demeanor.

"Calm down—there's no rush. Are you still drunk?"

"I'm not drunk! And this is me bein' calm!"

He'd become so agitated that he ran out of breath. He covered his face with his hands with a groan, needing a minute to calm his breathing. When he lowered his hands, his face seemed impassive, but in his eyes was a fiery look of earnest determination.

Schnell

"I'd given up hope long ago, or at least that's what I've been tellin' myself. Truth is, I can't give up my heart's desire. To me, blessweaving…"

He'd gotten so emotional that the words were getting caught in his throat. His fairy, who'd been watching him with keen interest, shuddered lightly, shedding the green magic she'd absorbed earlier. Argit could still see her as she became transparent, but even Endelia—to whom only dark fairies were visible—could sense the fairy's aura suddenly brimming with uncontrollable power.

They'd thought she was an ordinary fairy, except that she was very high-level, but the magic she'd exchanged with other fairies never stuck. When Amnart's and Hania's fairies made a consensual magical exchange, the magic they gifted each other didn't disappear or return to its original owner. Something very strange was going on with this wind fairy.

Seemingly oblivious to his fairy's transformation, Schnell spoke slowly, with great earnestness.

"Blessweaving is what I want to do more than anythin' in this world. I want to become a seamster."

The man Argit brought along froze when he saw me. Slowly, his eyes became as big as saucers, and he audibly gulped.

"…A-are you a fairy? A real live one?"

He reached toward me, tracing my silhouette with his hands as if to check that I was actually there.

"Black? White? Lace, but no primary colors. Pale tones. Silk stockings… A bird cage…," he muttered, breathing fast, eyes glistening with excitement.

To put it bluntly...he seemed like a madman. He was so handsome it was almost painful to look at him, which made his behavior even more unexpected and outlandish. That set off alarm bells for Mimachi, who stepped in between me and him, brandishing a knife.

"Get back, Lady Yui."

"Schnell, don't tell me you have a...special interest in young girls—?"

"I don't!" Schnell yelled, cutting off Argit.

He smoothed his clothes and assumed a more formal posture.

"*Ahem*... Please excuse my manners. I'm a friend of Arjet—I mean, Argit. My name's Schnell, and I'm an adventurer."

Schnell moved his left foot back, placed his right hand on his chest, and bowed elegantly like an aristocrat, but the expression on his face was very clearly saying "Oh, crap, I've done it now, no way am I gettin' out of this." I couldn't help giggling.

"Lady Yui...?"

"Don't worry, Mimachi."

Schnell's reaction to me reminded me of my own, when I saw myself in the mirror after my body's development caught up with my age.

"You're not...just an adventurer. You're an artisan... A seamster?"

My jailbait looks may have been a magnet for perverts, but they also served as an inspiration for craftspeople. Schnell's eyes weren't full of lust when he saw me. The movement of his hands when he traced my silhouette—was that him taking rough measurements? He forgot his manners because his mind was preoccupied with colors, outfits, and accessories which would suit me.

"How did ya...?"

Schnell opened his eyes wide. He looked so happy he might cry.

"Who are you? A fairy, for real? A divine messenger? How did ya know about me?"

Schnell

"I'm...a seamstress myself," I said with a smile, curtsying. "I'm Yui, Argit's Maiden of the Needle."

"......You made the clothes he's wearin'?"

"She did. Yui's my fiancée. We're getting married in a few months."

"Sounds like *you're* the one with a special interest in young girls!"

"......I'm pretty sure I told you I proposed to Yui in order to guarantee her safety."

Schnell and Argit spoke to each other casually, as if they were good friends. It made me smile.

I turned my attention to Schnell's fairy, tilting my head as I looked her up and down.

"Yui, I brought Schnell here hoping you might offer some insights about his fairy. This fairy's powers seem quite unusual even for one so high level—"

"Mr. Schnell...did you design her outfit?"

"Hm? Yeah, I did. Why d'ya ask?"

I heard shocked gasps around us.

"Hold on—Schnell! You can heal fairies, too?" Argit asked.

"Heal fairies? What are ya talkin' about?"

"You just said you made your fairy's outfit."

"*Designed* it, didn't make it. She liked my design, so she changed her outfit to make it look like that, simple." Schnell's eyes sparkled with sudden realization. "Wait... Miss Yui, you can sew garments for fairies?!"

"Wait a second, Schnell. Fairies don't just change their outfits on a whim!"

"What?"

"Their clothes are made from their magical power. They're a part of the fairy themselves! That's why they can't just... But you're telling the truth, aren't you? I didn't notice it before, because it didn't even occur to me it was possible, but your fairy's dress is different from when I first met you!"

"No way—fairies can't change the appearance of their clothes? Mine only decided to tag along because she liked my designs…"

True, most fairies couldn't change their outfits—the operative word being "most." But there were a few exceptions to the rule, one of which I witnessed fairly recently.

I'd crafted a garment out of magic, daringly revealing. The fairy liked it, but made some alterations—less revealing, yet somehow even sexier. Senri had buried her head in her hands when she saw it. That's right: The fairy in question was none other than Kairi.

If Schnell's fairy could also alter her clothes, that made three of them that I knew of—three, because Purple Prince could do it, too.

Purple Prince. Kairi, the king of sea fairies. And…

"The wind fairy…king."

◆

"What was that, Yui? The king of wind fairies?"

"Huh?"

Schnell was staring at me blankly. I cocked my head at him, puzzled that he hadn't figured it out.

"Ah… Did you think…fairies were only female?"

I extended my arm. Purple Prince jumped out of my shadow and sat cross-legged in my palm. Schnell squinted, scrutinizing him. Then he looked closely at his fairy beside him.

"My fairy……is a guy."

"Well, that explains it. Your fairy's not only high-level, he's a fairy king," Argit said, sipping tea.

We were sitting at a table, Argit next to me.

Schnell

"But you noticed it right away, Lady Yui," Endelia added with admiration.

"With practice...seamstresses can recognize...slight differences in body shape."

"Oh, of course! Lady Yui can make perfectly fitting garments without taking measurements, just by looking at someone. Recognizing a male body shape must be a trivial matter for her."

If seamstresses had various artisan skill levels, like in a game, maybe I had a skill that enabled me to do that. Although I had an eye for male and female body shapes even in my past life. My friends, and their friends too, used to ask me to make them costumes. Some of them were boys whose beauty would outshine most women, while others were girls who could easily pass for stunningly handsome guys.

Schnell, sitting across from us, was slumped over the table.

"For seven years... Seven whole years, I didn't notice..."

He was an artisan seamster himself, so it was a big shock which no doubt hurt his pride, but I didn't want to dwell on that. I was burning with curiosity about the contents of Schnell's bag, and the weapons at his belt.

"I'm mystified by the fact that both Schnell's wind fairy king and the newly born sea fairy king are so large, while Yui's dark fairy king is tiny. Why could this be?"

I was so transfixed by Schnell's belongings that I almost didn't register Argit was talking to me.

"Yui...?"

Argit touched my cheek with the back of his hand, concerned by my absent-mindedness. I finally looked up at him.

"Mr. Schnell...I've wondering about...your weapons, and the bag you've brought."

"Ah, that's right. Schnell brought that shirt to show you."

"I almost forgot. Sure, take a look."

The sight was so chilling, I got goose bumps all over.

"Eek…"

I instantly recognized that a curse had been woven into the garment with that putrid black and red thread. Fortunately, whoever made it was pathetically bad at sewing, so they stitched the front of the shirt to the back, making it impossible to put on.

Without waiting for a signal from me, Purple Prince drew his rapier and cut the cursed thread as though with a seam ripper.

"Oh…"

"Huh?"

The shirt came apart—unlike that awful garment of Argit's that Purple Prince had helped me cut, Schnell's shirt lost all semblance of a garment, turning into a pile of loose threads. Shiny particles of lucky blessing rose from it and disappeared into thin air.

"That… That could've ended badly!"

Having seen Aria's pink ribbon, I understood what had happened with the garment.

"It was almost…a perfect amulet. The curse…reversed its blessing!"

The only thing stopping the shirt from becoming an amulet was that its creator didn't consider it finished. An amulet would have repelled a curse like that.

"A what? Amulet?"

I slammed the table with my open hands.

"Mr. Schnell! Value your creations!"

"R-right!"

"Have confidence! It's because of your…self-doubt…that you didn't notice!"

The wind fairy king nodded, his eyes sparkling, smiling with relief.

He'd picked up Purple Prince in his hands and was rubbing his cheek against Prince's. Purple Prince didn't seem too pleased about this affectionate way of showing him gratitude, but he limply accepted it.

"The shirt I made…could've become an amulet?"

He brushed his fingertips against the pile of threads. Fat tears rolled down his cheeks. Poor Schnell—he really seemed to have trouble trusting his judgment, to the point that it altered his perception.

"Ha-ha… So, I've got nobody but myself to blame for it goin' to waste…"

The others waved their hands, telling the crying, defeated Schnell that it wasn't his fault.

"Not my fault? I didn't realize what I'd made!"

"Neither were we able to appraise it correctly. To us, it looked like a badly altered shirt with impure energy in those threads."

When Argit fell silent, I was the next to speak in my slow, halting manner.

"It was very lucky that…the person who wove the curse in…had poor needle skills. If you did put that shirt on…your body would have withered…and you'd have turned into a monster. Had the thread…acclimatized to the shirt…and fused with it…it'd have willed you to put the shirt on…"

He'd have turned into an undead, like a mummy.

"What do you mean about the thread acclimatizing?"

"The curse…is a living thing. Like the…former queen's curse…"

I broke into a coughing fit after speaking so much.

That thread was probably made by a human who'd turned into a monster, too. They tainted the magic stolen from fairies, turning its power from a blessing into a curse. It wouldn't even have been that powerful if it weren't for the shirt's amulet quality, which got flipped.

My throat was hurting, so I took out my notepad and wrote down my observations to show everyone.

"You'd have met an ugly end if the thread had adapted to the shirt and disappeared into it, making it wearable…"

"And it's a miracle that the curse became so strong, owing purely to the quality of the shirt Mr. Schnell had made."

"Not the sort of miracle anyone would wish for!"

"That cursed thread was stitched on by that Nuir pig! Is that guy breedin' monsters, or what?!"

Ah, of course it had to have come from my father. Aria had told me that at least one of my family's spiders was turning into a monster. I hadn't seen much of my father's and sister's spiders… Had my father fed a human to his? No, I couldn't believe it. My father was a horrible person, but he was only a third-rate villain. He abused those weaker than him without a hint of remorse, but he was a coward, without the gall to kill someone. Unless it was through indirect means, out of his sight—after all, he didn't explain to me or Rodin about the pact with the spiders, which could have led to tragedy. Had my spider turned into a monster because of that and killed people, I was sure my father would tell himself it absolutely wasn't his fault.

"That will have to be investigated. But before we move on to that, wasn't there something else of yours that attracted Lady Yui's attention?" asked Endelia.

Everyone's gaze drifted to Schnell's weapons at his waist. He unfastened the paper fan and placed it on the table.

"Wow, now, that's rare! A funky labyrinth weapon!"

Mimachi seemed fascinated.

"Paper fans aren't that unusual."

"I get hit with them all the time, but I've never seen one from a dungeon! And I've never met anyone who'd actually fight with one before! Metal ones, sure, but paper?"

"*Ahem*!" I swallowed a sip of tea and cleared my throat. "This isn't…a paper fan."

I was finding it hard to contain my excitement. Based on what Mimachi said, people didn't really use these fans, not knowing what they really were. Maybe there were loads of abandoned ones out there? I kind of wanted one for myself... Kind of wanted? Who am I kidding, I craved one!

"It's a weapon that...seamsters can...customize."

Schnell gasped, his eyes as big as saucers.

"Mr. Schnell, the fan is a base material. Look at it and...free your imagination."

I took a deep breath and exhaled slowly, and Schnell copied me, closing his eyes. After a few moments, he opened them wide again.

"The Fan of the Tengu King?"

He gasped again, looking at me. I nodded.

"If you can craft it well...it will become a powerful...wind weapon."

A wind weapon...with the severance effect, which was exactly what we'd been searching for.

CHAPTER 5

Apprenticeship

"A wind weapon? Ya sure?"

"As a rule of thumb, weapons found in labyrinths have properties suiting their owners, like His Highness's ice sword! Makes me wonder if other artisans who go on labyrinth expeditions also get weapons that don't seem like much but could be made into something awesome!"

Mimachi was trembling with excitement. She turned to me and Argit with a look of earnest supplication.

"Lady Yui! Your Highness! Do you mind if I get in touch with my people? There are many artisans among us with an adventuring side hustle!"

"You don't need to...ask me for permission," I told her.

"'Course I do! I can't pass on info from my mistress all willy-nilly!"

Surely none of this is groundbreaking intel, though? There must be other artisans who've figured out what the "dud" labyrinth weapons are for.

"Lady Yui, literally nobody I know would've thought of modifying a labyrinth weapon. Even people who can do it aren't going to try, because seeing a super rare dungeon treasure as a material for something else takes a monumental shift in perspective!" Mimachi added, as if reading my mind.

"Exactly," said Endelia. "Labyrinth weapons are considered to be weaker versions of mythic artifacts made by gods. Nobody would dare to try tinkering with an item imbued with mysterious, divine power, and we can safely assume that very few people would be capable of customizing such objects in the first place. Mr. Schnell here is a very good example."

"In that case, I think you should go ahead and pass this information to the Terra kingdom in person, Mimachi," said Argit. "It's located inside a labyrinth, after all. Despite the friendly relationship between our kingdoms, we haven't had the opportunity to do anything for you thus far, and I'd like to change that."

"Heh. There are precious few things in this world we Terra value more than good booze."

"And might I get in touch with you-know-who from the demon kingdom?"

"Of course. If Yui approves, that is?"

I nodded gingerly. I had a huge debt of gratitude to both Mimachi and Endelia, and if Argit thought international relations would benefit from sharing this information, that was fine by me.

"It's a pity Stolle and Senri have already left... But waiting even just one more day might have been too late, with the roads becoming unpassable."

The room filled with animated chatter, but Schnell was sitting in silence, still staring at me with big eyes as if he'd frozen from shock. Eventually, though, his gaze slowly dropped onto the weapon in his hands. He looked it over one more time, after which all emotion disappeared from his face. He stood up from his chair, walked over to me...and knelt on one knee, presenting me with the fan. Stolle had done the exact same thing once before!

Apprenticeship

Although it looked a bit funny when the object so formally offered to me was a paper fan.

"Sorry... Only the owner...can customize it."

Schnell shook his head.

"I'm not good enough yet. Which's why...I'd like to be yer apprentice!"

◆

Becoming a seamster wasn't that difficult. It didn't require any formal qualifications. As long as you could make clothes good enough to sell, you could call yourself a seamster.

"Thing is, I wanna make dresses."

"Hm...?"

"That's quite difficult for a man," said Endelia.

I cocked my head, not understanding.

"It's mostly the nobility that buys fancy dresses, but noblewomen have this aversion to letting any man know their sizes," Mimachi explained to me.

"I see..." Something else clicked in my head. "Mr. Schnell, were you once...a noble, too?"

No commoner would ever dream of making dresses for aristocratic ladies.

Schnell sighed, looking drained.

"Yeah. In another country."

He said he was from a small, faraway nation to the northeast, by the name of Calanquoia. Everyone but me looked shocked. I had never heard of this place.

"You've come a long way," said Argit.

"Had to travel somewhere that had no diplomatic relations with Calanquoia. I'm sort of a fugitive."

"Wait, what?" said Mimachi. "Wanted criminals aren't allowed to cross the border, though."

Schnell slammed his fists on the table, his face contorted in anger.

"Calanquoia is the reason I gave up on my dreams!"

"So you were framed for a crime you didn't commit?" asked Argit.

"I almost wish it'd been that, instead of somethin' so trivial…"

Schnell calmed down, his eyes glazing over as he began to tell us his tale.

Calanquoia is a small country located on the northeastern edge of the continent.

Schnell's family were high-ranking nobles, and he was their firstborn son. But no sooner had he taken his very first breath than it was decided he would never become the head of his house. Schnell had been born with a rare condition called hypermagicosis. His body stored more magic than it could safely handle, with no way of discharging it. Babies with this condition didn't live long.

For most people, the amount of magic naturally produced by their bodies was equal to the amount released, so that the amount stored remained at an equilibrium. But sometimes, that innate ability to self-regulate magic was impaired, causing either hypermagicosis or magic release disorder.

Hypermagicosis led to death from magic building up to toxic levels within the body. Magic release disorder was characterized by the body's inability to store magic, immediately releasing all of the magic produced. This, too, led to early death. Children affected by one or the other had very

slim chances of living to the age of ten, and none had been known to survive until twenty.

These hereditary conditions had apparently first appeared among royalty. I wondered if it had anything to do with consanguineous marriages which used to be common in royal families.

"Are you…still alive thanks to your fairy?"

"Yeah. I'm grateful for that, really am."

Schnell smiled warmly at the wind fairy king…but then he hung his head.

"He may be a dude, but to me, he's my goddess of salvation."

Schnell still couldn't get over the embarrassment of having mistaken his fairy king for a lady. I liked that it didn't lessen his attachment to his fairy, though.

Despite knowing that Schnell was unlikely to live long, his parents and grandparents celebrated his birth. They tried anything to prolong his life, even if only by a day—anything, including superstitions, such as bringing up the affected child as a different sex.

"I wouldn't have succeeded my father anyway, so with royal permission, I was brought up as a girl."

"Aha, so that was the missing piece!" said Argit. "I'd been caught off guard many times by how your manner would indicate you were of aristocratic blood, but something seemed odd. You were raised not as a noble, but as a noblewoman!"

Schnell clicked his tongue in annoyance.

"Anyhow… My parents decided to bring me up as a girl, keepin' me in the dark about the whole thing."

Schnell's parents reasoned that he was unlikely to live long enough for his body to take on a masculine appearance anyway, and it might distress him to present as a female if he'd known he was a boy, so they kept him believing he was a girl until he acquired his guardian fairy. The education he was given was typical of what noble girls would learn—including crafts such as sewing, which became Schnell's passion.

Not only Schnell's parents, but everyone who knew him encouraged him to pursue this interest, so that he might live out his short life in happiness. An accomplished older seamstress was hired as his tutor. Her warm personality and talent for passing on knowledge further kindled Schnell's fascination with sewing.

He was very happy back when he didn't know he was a boy. He loved making dresses for his pretty girl friends, even though his creations still looked very amateurish. His friends made him promise that he'd live long enough to make them wedding dresses. Surrounded by kind, supportive people, he worked on improving his sewing skills.

Then, one day, a powerful wind fairy found him.

Magic-related conditions, whether congenital or developed later in life, can be alleviated by fairies. From the day Schnell acquired his fairy familiar, he began to recover strength. Within a month's time, he was able to run around like any healthy child. His life was no longer in danger, and his fairy's wind affinity offered him another advantage as well.

A firstborn son with a fairy guardian would be guaranteed to become the successor to his noble house...unless his familiar was a wind fairy, and especially if that fairy was of a high level.

When a fairy of any other affinity decided to become someone's familiar, he or she could generally be trusted to stick with them through thick and thin, for as long as that person lived. This wasn't the case with the wind

fairies, who only stayed so long as their partner also enjoyed their freedom and followed their dreams.

Schnell's younger brother was already turning out to be an excellent candidate to succeed their father as the head of the house. Meanwhile, Schnell, brought up as a girl, was so happy that he'd have a full lifetime to devote himself to sewing. It was his dress designs which caught the eye of his fairy, too. His parents decided to reveal that he was in fact their son, not daughter, but let him carry on with dressmaking, and their decision was met with acceptance all around.

"When they told me I was a boy, I didn't know what to make of it at first, but the girls I'd been close with were true friends to me! They didn't cancel their orders, sayin' if my dresses won me over a fairy, they gotta be amazin'! And that when other women see them wearin' my designs, they too will want them, no matter that I'm a guy."

"Some might see it as an emasculating situation to be in, but if Mr. Schnell didn't have any strong feelings about his gender, his parents made the right call," Endelia muttered.

I tilted my head to the side, unable to think of a reason why Schnell would want to leave his country—based on what he was saying, after a bumpy start, he was living the life of his dreams.

He covered his face with his hands and continued the tale.

"Everythin' was fine…until one day, the youngest of the Calanquoia princes started demandin' I be his bride!"

"Huh?"

"He wouldn't shut up about it! I told him I was a guy! I told him I wanted to be a seamster! The bastard wouldn't listen!"

Even with his hands pressed against his face, Schnell's voice came out in a rumbling, resentful growl.

"Ah..."

Endelia made a little noise, as if something had just occurred to her. Argit closed his eyes, stroking his jaw pensively.

"Wasn't there an incident in that region several years ago involving a deadly disease that affected only men?"

"All but the youngest of the Calanquoia princes died from it, I heard...," Endelia added.

"Even the king caught that. He didn't die, but it took its toll on him, and he never fully recovered, forcing him to give up the throne," said Mimachi.

"At least that idiot prince made a good king. The disease eviscerated our kingdom, but he got it back in shape. He's a clever lad, actually, except for that nonsense about still wantin' to marry me!"

"That... That must be difficult for you."

As a man never having been in such a position, Argit seemed unsure of what to say.

"Difficult? You have no friggin' idea just what hell it was to me! He wouldn't give me peace, no matter how much I told him I had no intention of marryin' him! The youngest of the princes, he was a spoiled brat. Even before I got my fairy, when everyone was sure I'd die before long, some of his hangers-on would come badger me to marry him just for the few years I had to live! Can ya believe it?!"

Schnell kept shouting and explained that he rejected the marriage offers because he wanted to focus on honing his sewing skills. He then calmly sipped his tea.

"Did someone perhaps make an attempt on your life after that disease struck in your country?" Endelia asked, topping up Schnell's teacup.

"The crown prince had a fixation on you, and you had no interest in taking over as the head of your noble house... I can see why you might become a target," Argit said dryly, picking up a cookie.

As a royal, he was only too aware of how the issues of succession led to ugly plots and intrigues.

In our kingdom, only faysighted women were eligible to become queens, which limited rivalry between powerful noble houses. But in other countries, it was really vicious. Perhaps it was little wonder that Argit's second wife, a foreigner, lost her mind from jealousy.

"If that's all there was, I would've just carried on sewin' pretty dresses back in my country."

"You wouldn't be deterred by people trying to kill you…?"

I looked up at the wind fairy king. Schnell's condition caused his body to produce excessive amounts of magic, which his fairy was absorbing from him. To kill Schnell, the assassin would need to have his own fairy king with matching power. Even then, the wind fairy might have an advantage on account of its rare affinity.

"I guess Schnell doesn't have to worry about assassins," Mimachi said, arriving at the same conclusion as me.

"Worse than assassins was the faction tellin' that stupid prince he could make me his queen, as long as he had a female concubine to give him children."

"What…?"

Argit stared wide-eyed, his brain struggling to process this crazy development. My jaw dropped, and everyone else seemed just as thrown.

Slowly, anger began to thaw Argit's frozen expression.

"Despite your rejection of his advances?" he asked incredulously.

"Sounds to me like this faction's ulterior motive was to kill you," was Mimachi's take.

Forcefully installing Schnell as the queen, placing him under constant supervision, was sure to make his freedom-loving fairy leave, and without her, he'd be a sitting duck. An outraged murmur went through the room, but Schnell quickly silenced it.

"Nah, only a few people considered it. Most of them simply wanted to win the prince's favor."

"Are you sure about that?"

"Yeah. My fairy checked it for me. What a headache, eh?"

"Those people honestly wanted to pressure you into marrying the prince to get in his good books?"

"Yer forgettin' that outside of this country, people aren't very aware of fairies and what they do. In Calanquoia, people thought I luckily got cured by a fairy. I wouldn't have understood it either, if it weren't for the seamstress tutorin' me. She was from here."

While the others were still agitated, Endelia spoke coolly:

"Ah, of course. There are other countries where the inhabitants have a close relationship with the fairies, such as the demon kingdom I'm from, but you're from a small, remote place with mostly human population... I can see why they'd misinterpret your fairy's role."

"Yeah, even we Terra only know about earth fairies... No, wait, I lied. Specialized craftspeople learn about all fairy types."

I was a little confused. Hypermagicosis caused magic to accumulate in the sick person's body with no outlet, eventually causing their death. It sounded like a hereditary condition. Schnell's fairy was absorbing his magic, using it up or maybe just dispersing it—in any case, the fairy was regulating the amount of magic stored in Schnell's body, keeping him alive and well. So... Um...

"You said...they misinterpreted...what his fairy did?"

Was there any room for misinterpretation? It seemed rather straightforward to me. With his fairy regulating his magic for him, Schnell wasn't

Apprenticeship

experiencing any symptoms of his condition. If he lost his familiar, he'd start experiencing them again.

I wasn't the only one who seemed a bit lost—Argit and Mijit appeared perplexed as well. The three of us had never been abroad, so we were somewhat ignorant of the differences in what passed for common knowledge in other cultures. Experience from my previous life was of no help to me, since in that world, fairies were imaginary entities.

"It's like this, Lady Yui. People who don't know a dime about fairies would think, 'Wow, cool! This guy got a fairy, and his incurable disease just vanished! Fairy power cures people!'"

Mimachi's dumbed-down explanation left Argit, Mijit, and me gaping.

"It's partly down to the fact that the disease killed off a lot of men, leavin' survivors unable to work. The heads of many noble houses got replaced by youngsters too green for the job."

Schnell sighed heavily. I wondered why the topic suddenly changed away from the fairies, and why people in his country didn't seem to have any interest in them while they were so amazing and cute... Ah, that's right. Only the faysighted could see them.

"Yes, I imagine that led to quite a considerable social shift, but you said that the prince who was then made king was a capable ruler, irrespective of his foolish pursuit of you. Didn't he bring everything under control?"

"Everythin' except anythin' related to my family... After my fairy found me, other members of my household started gettin' fairy familiars, too. Nobody around me was fallin' sick anymore, which drew attention. Fools would turn up demandin' I hand over my fairy to them. I had to leave my homeland."

"Unbelievable..."

A similar thing happened at Rodin's household after my arrival. Schnell's household must have been full of good people, too. It made me angry to think the prince who claimed to be so in love with Schnell did nothing to protect him. Even if the prince had no ill intentions, he was terribly self-centered.

"So that's what you meant when you said you were a wanted man in your country."

Argit sighed deeply. As the former king, he'd refrained from asking about that earlier, perhaps because he'd be obliged to report a wanted criminal, if Schnell turned out to be one.

"Yeah. My brother and a few friends smuggled me out of the country several years ago. Since then, I've been makin' a livin' as an adventurer, lookin' for sewing work, too... No luck with that, though. No one's gonna hire a man who drifted from who-knows-where to sew dresses for highborn ladies."

Schnell gazed into the distance, bemoaning how it was precisely then that he realized that of all kinds of sewing work, dressmaking was his favorite.

"The old seamstress who taught me told me about the blessweaving performed by the Nuirs. She had a good opinion of the head of House Nuir, so I wanted to meet him, hopin' he might take me on as a dressmaker."

"She must have meant Yui's late uncle..."

"I get the picture now. You traveled here to meet the bigwig Nuir, and he turned out to be just a buffoon. To make sure, you commissioned that shirt, which he made a total mess of."

"Since that, I've been tryin' to find my tutor's twin sister, who she said was an even better seamstress than her. My tutor got adopted by a childless relative who worked as a peddler, then met her husband in Calanquoia,

where she settled. She couldn't remember her old family name, though, so it was kind of hopeless…"

"But then you saw me, dressed in the clothes Yui made for me. She lifted the curse from your shirt, revealing that it was an amulet, and that your labyrinth weapon can be customized. I see why you want to become Yui's apprentice."

Having heard his story, I had no objections to that. I nodded, taking his hand. By becoming my apprentice, he'd also gain the protection of Argit and Amnart. That's a big favor to owe someone for!

"I…accept you as my apprentice. In return…I ask you to help us!"

"Allow me to tell you about the quest we're on," Argit said. He took over explaining things from there.

And so, Schnell became my apprentice and a member of our team working to free the Realm Weaveguardian from the former queen's curse.

INTERLUDE

A Monstrous Spider

I didn't understand what had happened.

Father invited a dashing young man into the house. The man was slenderer than Nonnah Romiaccia, and he had downcurved eyes which made his smile look even more kindly. I thought he might be a prince in disguise, but he was supposedly an adventurer of common birth! What a pity—I prefer slim men to burly knights like Nonnah.

Still, he excited me, and I wanted to get closer to him, but Father shooed me away, saying he had something extremely important to talk about with that gentleman. I told him I'd go out on a walk then, but I crept up to the window of father's office and peeked inside. The curtains weren't fully drawn, so if I stood to one side of the window, I could see into the room.

I saw my father, his wonderfully enormous spider, and the spider's caretaker, that filthy spider handler woman. Why did she get to be there and not me? Wasn't it rude to the dapper guest to have that filthy woman in the same room? Or did the man come for her, the worthless spider handler, like when

Rodin Calostira arrived to take my weedy older sister? Even just thinking about it made me feel uneasy.

I glanced at my own spider, sitting on my shoulder. It'd grown pretty big, too—so big, carrying it around was hurting my shoulder. If Father was going to get a new spider handler, maybe he could get me one, too? I could blessweave, so I was special, but people didn't seem very aware of that. If I had a spider handler of my own, I could take my heavy spider with me wherever I went, and then everyone would pay attention to me, as they should. That idea cheered me up, but my joy was cut short by the spider handler's scream when that attractive man entered the room.

I was outside the house and the windows were closed, making Father's office soundproof, so how come I could hear her?

"Aaaaah! My dearest! You finally came to see meeeee!"

The man winced uncomfortably, which made me happy, because he clearly didn't like that dirty woman…except my knees were shaking. I didn't understand why, but that woman was really scaring me.

"You have a need for fresh fairy magic, you said?"

"I do! This one's useless! Not an ounce of magic in my spider's thread lately!"

Father kicked the spider handler. How come neither he nor the guest were afraid of her? I was so terrified it wasn't only my knees shaking anymore, but my whole body.

"I'm afraid I don't have any fairies to offer you at the moment. I had to release them in order to enter the country. As I explained to you when I brought her to you, vexingly, spells trapping fairies lose power when crossing the border of this country, and they also attract the border guards' attention."

"So what? This land is teeming with fairies. You've been here for quite some time. Why haven't you caught any?!"

"It's not as easy as it might seem, but I have good news. I've found a man you can use to draw out far more power than she could ever get you! But since he's a man, I can't lure him as I would a woman. Which is why I need your assistance."

"Is he the genuine thing, then? With a fairy familiar? Hmm... You need my help making him your slave?"

I was still watching from the outside, but I wasn't paying attention to Father and his guest anymore. My eyes were riveted to the spider handler, who slowly raised her head. Bloody tears were streaming from her eyes—which were no longer eyes of a human. They were all black with a dirty reddish sheen, without whites. They were spider eyes. She opened her mouth, widening from ear to ear, and slimy drool started dripping from between her fangs.

My shoulder felt heavy. Really heavy. I wanted to take a look at my spider, but I was too petrified with fear. I couldn't even cry out for help. The woman was scaring me as my parents and the maids did in the past, but this time, there was nobody there to comfort me. My big sister wasn't there to cuddle me tight and make me feel better. I wanted my sister...

The spider handler woman spread out her arms—her spider arms, which were half as long as the room she was in. And then...the men, who were within their reach, turned. They saw her, but there was nothing they could do.

"Aaargh!"

The guest's head disappeared in the woman's mouth with a sickening crunch. My father just stood there, dumbfounded. I also didn't understand what happened. I only knew that I'd witnessed something horrifying.

My shoulder felt heavy, and it hurt. I felt my spider stretch out its legs, like the spider woman did. And then I felt its claws digging into my shoulders and arms. Since when did it have claws? Claws so sharp...

I'm so scared! Oh, Yui, what should I do? Is this my punishment for not growing up to be the good girl you wanted me to be? I'm sorry, sorry for everything.

"Yui… Help me…"

There was a flash of light on my wrist. At first, I didn't know what it was, but then I saw that the friendship bracelet Yui secretly made for me with her spider's silk had snapped and was in pieces.

It was just a pretty little thing she made for me shortly after our parents separated us. There was no magic in it…but when that flash of light fell on my spider, it fell from my shoulder, also torn to bits. I felt something else snapping—it was my invisible link to the spider.

I collapsed onto the ground, next to my spider, overcome with sleepiness. I think that was a side-effect of our link breaking. My eyelids dropped shut.

I was saved. My sister saved me. Even after I'd been so horrible to her…

I'm sorry, Yui. And thank you. When I wake up, I will try to be a good girl you'd be proud of…

The truth is, I've been feeling out of sorts since our parents separated us.

I'd have been perfectly happy without Mother or Father, but I never wanted you to leave me, dear sister. It was you I loved the most. I still do. I wish I could forget everything except you…

CHAPTER 6

An Unexpected Connection

"After today, the hills will be unpassable. That's why the road's so crowded."

Gogol swore under his breath, following the long line of merchant caravans and carriages with his eyes. They were on the highway leading all the way to the royal capital.

"Also, everyone traveling to the capital has to take this route."

"It's already starting to snow a little," Senri noted.

"By evening, it'll likely turn into a blizzard," was Stolle's verdict.

Gogol let go of the reins, trusting the horse to stay on the path, and put on a waterproof coat.

"Aren't you ladies cold?"

Gogol had known Stolle for a long time; she was his master's girlfriend. She'd told him in the past that her armor was terribly cold in winter, unless she was moving around. She'd normally wrap herself tight in a thick, warm cloak to keep warm.

"Since Lady Yui awakened my armor, neither heat nor cold has any effect on me!"

Stolle leaned out of the carriage and caught some snowflakes with her gauntlet-covered hand, excited as if it was only now that she noticed her new resistance to frosty weather.

"All right, but what about you, Senri? She hates the cold. I saw her walking around the house with a blanket over her shoulders just the other day..."

Gogol turned to look at Senri, but he instead caught the gaze of the alluring male figure grinning and hovering next to her. The words died in his throat.

"It's snowing, but it doesn't really feel cold," said Senri.

"Right. I needn't have worried about you, what with your fairy fella."

"Ha-ha... Uh..."

Senri glanced up at Kairi and sighed. Yui had crafted him a new outfit, so he was wearing more than just a loincloth now, but he still turned heads. Having him around all the time was a pain in the neck.

"So we're stopping by my parents' home first?" Senri asked Gogol.

"Yep. Tangerine farmers, right?"

"Yes, but their farm is in the mountains. It's very remote. You can tell from the map I gave you yesterday."

"It's not that far, though. We'll only make a short stop there to pick up your portal repair tools and then get back on the road, so I reckon we'll reach the palace a week from now."

"A week? It's two days' journey from Senri's parents' if we take the backroads, making it four days total," said Stolle.

"Hold on, you're underestimating how treacherous the mountain paths can be! It's not winter in those parts, but there are no proper roads there, you know?!"

Senri didn't believe Gogol could get them to their destination a whole three days quicker than Stolle estimated.

An Unexpected Connection

"I know these roads well. I was a foundling, and my foster parents... I think they might be your grandparents, Senri."

""Whaaat?!""

Gogol stared into the distance.

"I was just one of many foundlings Michinaga and Riou raised together. I wasn't a special case."

"I remember being told my grandparents operated an orphanage in another country..."

"I was the last foundling they looked after before moving back here."

Gogol became independent and moved out as soon as he became an adult. Senri's parents got married around that time. He'd heard they had a daughter, but he didn't know her name.

"Did you maybe recommend Master Rodin to my parents when I decided to become a maid?"

"I didn't, but they knew from me that he was a reputable employer. They didn't tell me you'd be coming to work there. I suppose they didn't want me doting on you."

Senri took a good look at Gogol, noticing for the first time that he wasn't much older than her. Could he be the young uncle who was the talk of her village back in the day?

"Are you the uncle who became a famous adventurer and moved out of the village to travel the world?"

"No, that's my older brother. I wonder what he's doing these days."

"Ah, okay..."

She was relieved it wasn't him. Everyone used to draw unwelcome comparisons between her, with her beastly strength, and that famous uncle. Even though he obviously had no idea how he became a major cause of stress for her, if she'd actually met him, she might fly into a fit of rage, and that would be very embarrassing for her.

"Anyway, the mountains where your parents live are enchanted. There are shortcuts only the Kamioka family can take."

"The mountains are enchanted?!"

"You've only ever gone there in the village coach, right? For a Kamioka, it's less than a fifteen-minute walk from the foot of the mountain to your village."

"No way! You can't get up that steep cliff that fast! And what about the rope bridge?"

"For the village coach, it's tricky, but I can get this carriage to your parents' home in no time at all. Lady Stolle will have to wait at the foot of the mountain, though."

Gogol paused, thinking.

"Hmm, it'll be faster to take the byroad on foot. Lady Stolle, will it be okay if we leave you with the carriage? It won't be a long wait."

"That will be fine... I'm astonished that a spell could be cast over the entire mountain range, though."

"Doesn't seem so unusual to me? I've only ever seen Riou's magic at work, though, so I can't really compare."

"Yes... I can believe Grandmother could do that..."

The three sighed.

"Michinaga and Riou have a divine connection, right?"

"As their foster son, you also have a connection to the gods, no? Although I suppose you wouldn't be authorized to travel through portals."

"I still haven't even gotten used to thinking that my grandparents and dad have special powers! It's too much new information all at once!"

Stolle took in the view from the foot of the mountain. The village where Senri's parents lived was a long way from where she was. She could make

An Unexpected Connection

out a small group of buildings on the mountainside, farther than halfway up but not that close to the orange peak.

Besides protection from heat and cold, Stolle's awakened armor also improved her vision. Even before the awakening, it granted her the power to see through obstacles, but now it also allowed her to easily find and focus on what she wanted to see. She'd only noticed it recently. This power was not without limits, though—she quickly lost sight of Gogol, Senri, and Kairi when they entered a secret path leading through a thicket.

They had traveled on the main road for two days, after which they took the byroads until they reached the mountains. Gogol halted the carriage at the foot of the mountain.

"All right, we'll do the rest on foot."

"What, from here? This is crazy..."

They left Stolle and the carriage, picking their way through bushes on a trail so overgrown it might not have been a trail at all, not even one used only by wild animals. According to Gogol, that's where the magical shortcut was.

A magical shortcut—Gogol made it sound uncomplicated, but Stolle couldn't understand quite how that worked.

There were different kinds of magic in this world. One of them was the magic of the fairies, and another was the magic of humans and non-human people, which was a power their bodies generated naturally, and which could affect the physical world. The third kind of magic was a mixture of the two, called magecraft.

According to old folktales, in the distant past, fairies were more ethereal, ephemeral beings without any magic at all. The only magic in existence back then was that made by people, but it gradually disappeared. People lost the ability to cast powerful spells.

Magic used to be a powerful weapon used against monsters. Without it, people couldn't defend themselves, and monsters began to take over. This upset the world balance, prompting a divine intervention—the gods turned the rare fairies flickering in and out of existence into proper dwellers of this world.

Based on what Gogol said about Senri's grandmother, her magic was unusually powerful. He'd never been among magicians, so his only points of reference were Senri's grandparents. To him, what they could do was the standard, but they might have both wielded a power beyond belief.

The mountain had a cute name—Tangerine Peak—but there was nothing cute about the mountain range it was a part of. On the other side, there was a twisty road which was just about manageable. Approaching from where Stolle had been left waiting seemed foolish at best. The trail went up at a steep angle, up tall cliffs where the rock face was almost vertical at times. It was incredible to think that Senri's grandmother made it possible for her family to climb up that way with ease, and that her magic would linger even when she was no longer in the vicinity.

"Just how powerful was she...?"

Senri's grandparents passed on the task given to them by the gods to their daughter and her husband, and they moved back to their homeland. Yui had guessed what the basis for their authorization to use the portal was, and the entity supervising the portals, by the name of Guide, kept her temporarily captive for that reason. Senri came from a family with special ties to the gods, which entitled her to use the portals, but why was Yui entitled to use them, too? Whatever it was, Stolle hoped it didn't put Yui in danger.

As if summoned by her anxious thoughts, Yui appeared before Stolle's eyes. She was sketching something on paper and happily talking to a man Stolle had never seen before. The next moment, Stolle's field of vision was almost entirely filled by the face of a fairy. Even at a glance, it was clearly a very high-level fairy.

"A fairy? How's this possible?"
A chill ran down Stolle's spine.

Stolle didn't have faysight, but she was looking at a fairy...who was looking back at her! And how was it possible for her to see Yui, who was far, far away? Confusion and fear welled up in Stolle's chest.

Snap!
Something hit Stolle lightly, and she blacked out.

"It really was a shortcut..."
Senri's mouth hung open in astonishment when they emerged in the village.
"Didn't believe me, huh? Anyway, you need a carriage to get to the start of the trail at the bottom of the mountain, so you can't come and go without me."
They were in a tangerine orchard about halfway up the mountain. The familiar sight of ripe, bright-orange tangerines made Senri realize she'd missed home.
"Your parents' house is that way, right?"
"Yes… Um, Gogol? The trail has disappeared…"
The path they'd followed was nowhere to be seen. She needed no more proof that it was magical.
"Don't worry. When you want to head back down, just go into the woods and you'll find it again."
"If you say so…"
They started walking through the orchard, and before long, they saw a house. There were two people waiting on the porch.

An Unexpected Connection

* * *

"Welcome home!"

One of them was a young man, who at a closer look was breathtakingly handsome, yet strangely, he easily faded into the background. His hair was golden and eyes very dark brown like Senri's, although that was as far as the similarities went. Kanhe, as that was his name, was Senri's father.

Next to him stood a girl as pretty as a doll. Well, she looked like a young girl, but was in fact Senri's mother, Mari. Her baby face and petite build made one wonder whether she had some Terra blood in her. Mari's long hair was black, her eyes obsidian, skin an ivory white. Senri had a complex because of her lack of resemblance to her parents.

Other children in the village would tease her about being a foster child. The one good thing that came out of her recklessly using that portal was meeting her grandparents and seeing that it was them she'd taken after.

"H-hello! Um… You came out to greet us? How did you know we were coming?"

"Mari said it was time to pack our bags."

Kanhe glanced to the side, to where their travel bags were on the ground. Senri hung her head, feeling herself no match for her mother's intuition.

"We should make haste and go to the palace at once," Mari said.

"Something sinister is brewing," Kanhe added.

"What do you mean by 'sinister'?"

"Well, if everyone's ready to go, let's go. We don't want to keep Lady Stolle waiting too long."

"Right…"

Senri's rare visit to her home village was over in just ten minutes.

◆

They weren't prepared for what they saw when they descended the mountain. Stolle wasn't waiting for them next to the carriage. She was lying in the dirt as if someone had pushed her over.

Gogol and Senri ran over to her in a hurry.

"L-Lady Stolle?!"

"Lady Stolle!"

Stolle wasn't the type to nod off and fall over. Gogol quickly checked if anyone was hiding near the carriage.

"You don't think someone attacked her, do you?"

"Don't shake her, Senri."

"I'm trying to wake her up, Dad!"

"Let Mom take a look at her first."

Kanhe, who'd been carrying Mari in his arms, sat her down next to Stolle. She held her hand over Stolle's mouth briefly. When she reached to remove Stolle's helmet, Senri stopped her.

"Mom, no! Lady Stolle is forbidden from removing her armor in front of any man until she marries! It's her family tradition!"

"Is that so?"

Mari's face remained expressionless, but she let go of the helmet and instead brushed the back of her hand against it. She looked up at Kairi.

"I sense traces of energy similar to your fairy king's."

"Whaaat?! Kairi, did you do something to Lady Stolle?!"

"I did not."

Kairi pouted at her and drifted over to Stolle. He touched each part of her armor with his fingertips before giving his verdict.

"The armor fairy is unconscious."

"Hmm... She's a half-air fairy, from what I can see. I'm guessing it was the wind fairy king who knocked her out."

"Air fairies possess the Limitless Gaze ability. They can show people

An Unexpected Connection

anyone or anything they wish to see. It seems your friend accidentally peeked at the wind fairy king."

"Did that fairy king hurt Lady Stolle?"

Before Senri's mother could answer, Kairi impatiently cut in.

"No, she's fine."

"Indeed. Like her fairy, she has merely lost consciousness."

Gogol looked at Senri.

"His Highness went to see some adventurer who has a wind fairy, no?"

"That's what he said...," she replied, meeting his eyes.

They both sighed with relief.

"Lady Stolle was probably wishing she could see if Lady Yui was safe..."

"Yeah. She must've been worried about leaving her with Mimachi. The housekeeper and Luroo are with her, but she may be thinking that's not enough."

"I personally think Lady Yui can keep Mimachi in line without any help."

"I guess. It helps that she's completely indifferent to Mimachi's behavior."

"Yui is the girl you're looking after, Senri dear? The girl with the dark fairy king as her familiar. And she's in the company of someone with the wind fairy king. That's some illustrious company. She must have quite the charisma."

"Darling, Yui's charisma is average. It's the former king's charisma at work here. But Gogol's master outshines even him in that respect," Mari said with a little ladylike laugh as her husband picked her up into his arms again.

"How can you know Lady Yui's stats when you haven't even seen her, Mom?"

Senri looked at her mother, ensconced in Kanhe's arms, with a shudder.

"Don't give me that look, Senri. The armored lady swore lifelong service to the little seamstress, didn't she? I can sense this and that about the people she's connected to. She has as her guardians both Gogol's master, whose talents alone could make him a splendid king, and the former king, the one without much luck in love matters. It's thanks to them that she's surrounded by powerful people."

Mari booped Senri's nose and lifted her gaze to the sky.

"We'd better be on our way. Senri, carry the armored lady to the carriage. Lay her down in the cargo space."

"It's going to rain soon, hmm?" Kanhe said, and Mari nodded. "Gogol, will you get the waterproofs out?"

Senri and Gogol did as they were told in a hurry, and soon, they were back on the road.

"Mom, you said earlier that Master Rodin could become a great king?"

Gogol went over the roster at Rodin's residence in his head, rubbing his temples. As the coachman, he had a good handle on where everyone serving in the household was from and what race they were. It hit him that Rodin had a lot of staff of exceptional ability, unusual bloodlines, and rare races.

"He has the potential, but it is not a path he desires to tread. Which is why neither the former nor the present king see him as a threat. And to him, they are allies, not rivals."

"I'd like to also add this... You two think yourselves the most common in Rodin's household, don't you? But you, Gogol, are a foster son of Michinaga and Riou. And you, Senri, are their granddaughter, and you have us as your parents. Which makes you both the most overpowered."

"What?" Senri and Gogol asked in unison.

CHAPTER 7

Sacred Tree

At the Nuir residence, Amnart wove a barrier of thorny vines of flames around his allies. There was the captain of the royal guards, Luluah Romiaccia. Next to him, Hania, Amnart's fiancée. Behind them, the old butler Welus. They'd been joined by the tangerine farmers, Kanhe and his wife Mari. They reached behind them and drew an exquisite white and a black sword, respectively, out of thin air.

Beside Amnart was Rodin's boss—Kayana Kamioka, a senior official of an advanced age, in a wheelchair. She waved a tangerine twig at the others.

"Good luck, everyone!"

Her cheering was a bit comical, but Kanhe and Mari gave her a little wave before heading in.

"I'm going in, Am."

"Please be careful, Hania."

She followed after the farmer couple. Amnart could only pray for her and the others' safety.

The magical adviser Toluamia Mishutu was being driven around in a carriage by Gogol to stick tangerine branches in all four corners of the residence grounds.

When Mari informed the king that she sensed one of the Nuir spiders had turned into a monster, several of the members recruited for the battle against the former queen's curse were called.

The spider monster had begun reproducing, so they had to act swiftly to prevent the spiders from spreading out of the Nuir residence and possessing other people. They were chosen for their resistance to possession by the spiders. The king's informers who had been keeping an eye on the Nuirs had to leave due to their lack of such resistance. Welus grinned, thinking about the draconian training he was going to subject them to until they built up their monster defense.

Neither Stolle nor Senri were there. Stolle hadn't yet awakened, and Senri couldn't fight. Kairi might've been useful in the battle, but he had no intention of leaving Senri to go and help someone else. They were staying at the palace together with Rodin and the vice-captain of the royal guards.

Senri was probably carrying the mythic artifact her mother gave her to the portal she was to repair, her knees shaking from nerves.

"I wish I could fight on the front line…," Amnart muttered ruefully.

He knew he had his own important part to play, though.

Before Amnart's party faced the Nuir spider monster, Senri's parents—entrusted by the gods with the task of releasing the original Nuir spider—paid a visit to Rodin's office in the capital instead of Stolle, who was still unconscious. As they got close to the palace, they both screwed up their faces.

"There's a powerful curse at work here, yes."

"This bad energy is coming from none other than the Realm Weaveguardian. The Nuir spiders are not unrelated."

"I see what you mean, dear. The Nuirs let their land be corrupted, making the Realm Weaveguardian vulnerable to curses."

Mari blinked twice and her dark eyes began emitting a pale blue glow.

"Um, what was that, Mom?"

"Activating skill Star Reading."

Senri used to think the only unusual thing about her parents was their looks, and aside from that, they were ordinary tangerine farmers. Seeing her mother using strange powers and saying strange phrases she'd never heard before was too much of a shock, making her wish she could just dissociate from reality.

Skills were special abilities which could be innate or acquired following certain experiences. Some of them worked without the person expending any magic at all, while others had a small magic cost—and those had to be activated with a special phrase. The majority of the population didn't have any skills at all, and among those who had innate skills, most wouldn't have realized it, unless someone with the ability to sense others' skills told them what they could do. Very, very rarely, extremely gifted people managed to awaken their dormant skills without anyone's help.

"Dad, what does Star Reading do?"

"It allows a glimpse into the near future with high probability."

"So Mom has other skills besides Appraisal?"

Senri knew her mom had that skill but believed it to be something used to determine the sugar content in tangerines.

Kanhe flashed a little smile at her but didn't answer her question. Senri was beginning to really feel out of her depth.

"I see…a sacred tree."

Mari's eyes returned to normal. Kanhe turned to Rodin.

"Lord Calostira, could you please ask your supervisor Kayana to come see us?"

"My boss? But... Oh, don't tell me you're related? Her surname is Kamioka, like yours..."

"She's my wife's foster sister."

Rodin stared at Mari, who was in her forties but looked like a young girl. Her foster sister was supposedly not even forty yet but looked like an elderly woman. How did that make sense?

Amnart was very fond of Kayana, his chief civil servant who had been born with a disability making her unable to walk. He was in her office when Rodin came to get her.

Rodin told Amnart about his company—a maid with a fairy who had a physical body, and her parents, on an important mission given to them by the gods, who were Kayana's relatives. Amnart did his best to appear unfazed. When Rodin said they also needed to talk to him about the Nuir curse, the king agreed to see them at once. They headed to the audience room, with Amnart pushing Kayana's wheelchair. Despite the suddenness of the other Kamiokas' visit, there was no discernable change in Kayana's calm manner.

"Brother, sister, it's good to see you," she said to them.

Kayana was covered in wrinkles, and her hair held in a bun with a hair stick was all white except for one green streak. Her eyes were a green so dark it was almost black. They glimmered with deep wisdom, but her heavy, deeply creased eyelids almost hid that from view.

She was one of the few female senior palace officials who remained in office throughout the former queen's reign.

Kayana was Mari's foster sister and Kanhe's sister-in-law, but she was clearly much older than them. Amnart delicately asked about it.

"Your Majesty, forgive me for having kept this secret from you, but I'm from the treefolk race. I may seem old to you, but I'm still merely a sapling," she explained.

It had never occurred to Amnart that she might be a half fairy, and that was why she couldn't walk.

The treefolk would normally put down roots in their homeplace and never leave it, which is why there hadn't been any records of them in Lomestometlo Kingdom. They were as rare as the giants.

Nobody would have guessed that this senior palace official in a wheelchair was but a young maiden. She'd intentionally given herself a wrinkled appearance.

Mari gave Amnart some time to process this new information before speaking to him.

"Your Majesty Amnart Lomestometlo, it is a pleasure to make your acquaintance. My name is Mari Kamioka, and this is my husband, Kanhe. The gods have sent us here with an important mission."

There were several unbreakable rules in this world, per the gods' design. Those with money-creating skills could not use their powers for illicit purposes. Those with the Appraisal skill could not lie about what the skill let them see. And nobody could misinterpret themselves as a messenger from the gods.

That's why everyone could instantly tell when money was counterfeit, even without Appraisal. And it was physically impossible for anyone to say they were on a mission given to them by the gods if it wasn't true.

"Our mission is to release the Nuir founder's spider and restore the palace portal. This is why we have traveled to the capital, but we've noticed that another matter needs to be urgently resolved before we can focus on our task—a Nuir spider has reverted into a monster and must be exterminated."

Amnart hurriedly sent out summons to his battle party members who'd been on standby especially for this eventuality.

* * *

"And you're thinking of having Kayana take part in this battle…?"

While Kayana avoided hostility and attacks during the periods of instability at the royal palace, having cleverly assumed the appearance of an old lady, she was a court official, not a fighter. Amnart couldn't picture her as a monster slayer.

"I must again apologize for the lack of transparency, but I have been working here only to facilitate the execution of our family's mission from the gods," Kayana confessed with an easy nonchalance.

"What…?"

"My role was to get in touch with Mari in the case of Nuir spiders reverting to monsters, causing their downfall, as well as to assist with the installation of the gate management system. We acted under the assumption that the Nuir spiders' turning into monsters would not suffice to grant release to the original spider. After the death of Yui's uncle, who was the last of the righteous Nuirs of his generation, my grandparents passed on their divine mission to their children. I entered service at the palace to have access to all the information I needed to fulfill my role."

"The spiders' reversal to monsters wouldn't free the original spider…?"

"My foster parents weren't expecting to discover a way to awaken the original spider and grant her complete release. We've been hard-pressed to come up with a solution to this problem."

"Our earlier plan was for Kayana to feign her death once House Nuir had fallen, so that we'd be allowed entry into the palace grounds to collect her body and personal belongings. Which would give us the chance to carry out our mission."

"Miss Kayana, please don't leave us! Without you, the rest of us palace officials won't cope!" Rodin implored.

Amnart nodded gravely.

"I'm sorry to have to leave so soon after Your Majesty's coronation. I've been making arrangements for a suitable replacement in secret, but I'm afraid I don't have anyone ready just yet."

"That's a matter to discuss another time. I have performed Star Reading. We will need Kayana for her skills and advantages that come with her race, that is certain."

◆

The treefolk had a natural ability to control nearby flora and to boost others' powers related to growing plants. With Kayana's support, Amnart was able to surround the entire Nuir residence with his thorny vines of flames.

Initially, the king was to take part in the battle for practice before facing the curse of Lestlana, but Mari advised that he should stay back and keep up the defense around the residence in order to stop any of the spiders from escaping.

If it were Yui's father who had fallen prey to the monster spider, it wouldn't have been as big of a problem, but Mari saw with her skill that it wasn't him, but a woman he'd been keeping in captivity that fused with the spider. She was similar to the former queen Lestlana in character, and the curse resonated with her. When she ingested the man she'd been obsessed with, the curse amplified her power, turning her into a high-level monster…and she began to reproduce. Had even a single spider managed to escape and hide somewhere, it could spawn more, which would be disastrous.

Amnart's visage was stony, his mind weighed down by the enormous responsibility.

"You needn't worry, Your Majesty. They can take care of it."

"I don't doubt they will, and yet…"

Amnart sensed something.

* * *

"Ah…"

It seemed to him as if the air shimmered for a moment. He turned toward the main building of the Nuir residence in the distance.

"It has begun, hasn't it?"

"Yes."

"Gogol has finished circling the grounds. Your Majesty, the preparations to purify this land are complete."

"Please proceed."

Kayana stuck a tangerine twig into the dirt.

"You're a good twig, a twig of the tangerine tree, created by the gods as the most sacred tree of all," she chanted.

The twig rooted in the ground and began sprouting a tall, thick trunk.

"You're a good tree, the tangerine tree, created by the gods overcome with desire for your fruit."

Kayana bent over the sapling, which grew faster, creaking and crackling, sprouting branches, leaf buds opening and leaves unfurling. Her legs fused with the tree, and despite his internal resistance, Amnart had to accept that she really was a treefolk.

The hunched Kayana straightened her back, supported by the trunk of the tree. Her wrinkles straightened out as she shapeshifted into a beautiful young woman.

"I am a good tree, the tangerine tree. I, who have grown as a nutmeg-yew, am permitted to be grafted onto the sacred tangerine. I am a good tree; I am the sacred tree!"

* * *

Kayana, the tangerine tree she was now a part of, and the ground all around began to glow. Amnart knew it was time. He knelt in front of the tree.

"I, Amnart, the King of Abundance, hereby ask the sacred tree to purify this land!"

Instantly, the glow spread in all directions.

"Activating skill Sacred Tree Transformation," Kayana whispered softly.

◆

"She activated her amulet. This raises her chances by fifty percent," Mari said, looking at a girl lying on the ground.

Kanhe understood she meant the girl's probability of being saved.

"I've appraised her. She's a blank slate."

"That's Meilia Nuir!" said Hania, who'd just caught up to them.

"Her name is now Mei. Her pact with her spider has been broken."

Hearing her name, perhaps, the girl shuddered, wincing.

"Huh?"

Hania watched as color drained out of Mei's hair.

"She's no longer Meilia Nuir…?"

She did look like a different person to Hania, with hair faded to gray and no gaudy makeup.

Welus joined them. He examined the remains of a spider next to Mei.

"Her spider had become a monster, too, but it's dead."

He noticed the torn friendship bracelet with surprise. He picked it up for a closer look.

"This is the first time I'm seeing an amulet with its power spent."

"This type can only be activated when its owner has a special bond with its creator," remarked Kanhe.

The royal guard captain Luluah suddenly appeared beside them without making a noise, despite his heavy armor.

"Did you hear that scream? It came from the residence!" he shouted.

He ran to the main entrance, but stopped in his tracks when the ground began to glow. The party turned around and saw a lush, majestic tree towering over a sickly-looking corpse.

"Like in the fairy tales…"

"Kayana has some very impressive skills."

"Is that a sacred tree?" Welus asked, in awe.

Kanhe tapped his shoulder.

"Could you take this girl to Kayana?"

"I must stay with Lady Hania to protect her…"

"Welus, please. She's no longer a Nuir. Her activating the amulet proves that she's worthy to live in this world, to be a citizen of this kingdom. While I'm not a king, I'm destined to become one. And it is the duty of the royalty to protect innocent citizens."

"Besides my husband and I, the fire-wielding maiden is the strongest against the spiders. She needs no protection," Mari added.

"And you are quicker on your feet than the guard captain."

They heard the windows shattering, and soon a deluge of spiders as big as a child's hand poured out of the house. Hania slammed her fists together, and sparks flew out to surround her.

"Welus! Take the girl and run!" she ordered in a mighty voice.

Welus could not ignore her order. He picked up the unconscious Mei and broke into a run.

* * *

"...Heh."

Welus grinned, running at great speed, his mad grin strangely out of place for an old, sagacious butler.

He was a butler, supporting the royal family from the shadows. That's what he'd been raised to be, right from the moment he was born. He was a man of exceptional talents, and consequently, he would not serve anyone he didn't deem worthy. It was only the most outstanding of royals that he would bow to, bend his knee, and pledge lifelong service. Thus, he chose Argit and Amnart. He considered himself fortunate to have found two worthy masters, while many butlers lived their lives ordered around by mediocre men. He didn't expect to ever take orders from anyone else.

"How exhilarating! When she commands me, my whole body tells me to obey! Ha-ha-ha!"

Welus was no longer the king's butler. He felt as if he'd been reborn, and his new incarnation was that of the future queen Hania's most powerful guardian.

◆

The spider of the former head of House Nuir, Yui's father, had fused with the woman the Nuirs kept as a slave, and with Yui's father as well—his body was partially assimilated into the spider's side, making for a horrifyingly ugly sight. It had become a powerful monster, rivaling or perhaps even exceeding the physical manifestation of the former queen's curse, and it was busily producing more and more spiders.

Strong as it might be, when the battle party entered the room after the

Kamioka couple, the spider was already in pieces, with all eight legs cut off. Kanhe snapped his fingers and the monster's remains caught fire, burning down to ashes. He and his wife were truly overpowered.

The rest of the team took care of the newly hatched spider monsters.

"Of course they're on a whole different level from the rest of us. The gods wouldn't have entrusted them with a mission otherwise," muttered the royal guard captain Luluah.

Meanwhile, at the palace, a portal room had been set up in the room where Senri had been waiting with Rodin for her parents' return.

The moment the last of the Nuir spider monsters had been slain, the original spider was freed from both her pact with the Nuirs and her role as the palace portal guardian. Momentarily, a mythic artifact for configuring the portal appeared in the room. Senri hadn't been expecting that—she thought she was only going to be waiting there with the tools her parents had given her until their return—and she got so stressed, she broke down into tears. Rodin did what he could to help her calm down, and, crying, she completed the portal setup following voice instructions from Guide.

At a glance, it was just an empty room, but activating the portal would make a magic circle light up on the floor.

When her parents finally got back, Senri threw herself into their arms, tears streaming down her face.

"You told me to just wait in the room! You never mentioned I'd be doing the use authorization setup!"

Senri's grandparents had asked her specifically to take care of the portal, and she was prepared to use it to travel by herself, but when the god-made mythic artifact appeared before her eyes, she got cold feet.

Her parents were, of course, used to her confidence swings and didn't feel the need to offer her words of sympathy. Mari spoke directly to Guide,

making sure that the setup had been completed without any problems. It was then that Senri put two and two together and realized that if she was authorized to use the portals due to her lineage, so was her mother. Also, her mom seemed very familiar with interacting with Guide.

"Er... Mom, you can use the portals, too?"

"Yes, darling. Well, our work here is done."

"Couldn't you stay and help us prepare for the battle with the curse of Lestlana?" asked Luluah.

The couple had made short work of the fearsome Nuir spider monster, so the royal guard captain was keen to train under them.

"I'm afraid not. As much as we'd like to help you free the Realm Weaveguardian from the curse, Ariadne wishes for people from this country to take responsibility for what happened. We're outsiders, and besides, I will soon be having a baby."

"You'll what?!"

Senri stared at her mother's belly, without any sign of roundness, wondering if she'd misheard.

"My husband Kanhe is a dragonkin, so I'll be laying an egg. You'll have a little brother or sister, Senri."

"You'll be laying an egg?! And also, Mom! You've been fighting while you're preg—um, about to lay?!"

"I swung my sword a few times; I wouldn't even call that a battle. But soon I will enter a state much like hibernation until it's time to lay. During that time, your father will become singly focused on looking after me. We won't be able to assist you."

"It was like that when Mari was preparing to lay your egg, too, Senri. Your mother will be hibernating for a year, and you cannot wait that long to exorcise the curse."

"A *year*?!"

Senri didn't know that she'd hatched from an egg, either. Since she had become authorized as a portal user, it seemed as if everybody around was coming out with jaw-dropping revelations, and she couldn't keep up.

"The amount of time it takes from conception to the egg-laying period varies greatly, and my skills don't work on myself. I discovered it would soon begin when I peered into the future to see about the palace curse."

"Ahhh, when you used Star Reading! I'm so happy! We'll be having another baby soon!" the usually quiet Kanhe bellowed happily, beaming.

Kanhe's joyful roar pushed Senri's head back like a gust of wind. Everyone except the still-unconscious Stolle, Kairi, and Kayana—back in her wheelchair but with a radiantly youthful appearance—covered their ears. It wasn't deafeningly loud, but a force pushed their heads back while their bodies were rooted to the spot, and the world seemed to be spinning in front of their eyes.

"It's...magical intoxication." The magecraft adviser Toluamia worked it out.

Kanhe's voice was brimming with powerful magical force, and they absorbed it just by hearing it.

"Kanhe, *shh*!"

Mari pressed her index finger to his lips, and Kanhe, flustered, covered his mouth.

"I haven't heard my husband raise his voice in a long time. It has quite the impact."

"Well, I suppose you should return to the mountains without further delay?" asked Gogol, the first to recover.

He went over to the palace garden-facing window and opened it at Kayana's instruction. Kanhe's face was colored with uncontainable excitement. He picked up his wife in his arms and headed for the window. His pupils stretched vertically, short hair elongated to halfway down

his back, and pink horns reminiscent of a deer's appeared on both sides of his head. His presence was so overwhelming, it was hard to believe this was the same person as the quiet, self-effacing man they'd known him as. He stepped over the window ledge and floated in midair.

"Please excuse us, but we must leave you now."

"Wait… I haven't given you your reward for the battle yet!" Amnart shouted, breaking out of the dizzy spell.

But the tangerine farmers only waved at him and flew away into the distance.

CHAPTER 8

And Then

When Mei woke up, she didn't know where she was. She looked around, her eyes turned ashen gray, like her hair—but she hadn't seen herself in a mirror yet, and she wouldn't have remembered that her hair and eye color used to be different anyway.

"Where am I…?"

The room seemed to be sparkling, but maybe it was just in her head? She was feeling so tired, she couldn't even sit up.

"I… I don't remember what happened…"

She had a vague feeling that she'd been somewhere very scary not long ago, but the room was neat and not scary at all. It was all very puzzling.

"Mei… My name's Mei…"

The only thing she could remember with some degree of clarity was someone gently stroking her hair, saying "You're a good girl, Mei" in a kind voice.

"My name…is Mei."

The person with the kind voice must have rescued her from the scary place! She couldn't remember it, but that's what must have happened!

"Oh, you're awake, Miss?"

A woman had entered the room, and her voice was kind, too, but it wasn't the voice she remembered. There was something sparkly about it, just like the room.

"Good morning...?"

"Good morning. Finally, color has returned to your cheeks."

"I...don't remember much. I only know my name's Mei..."

"Mei? That's a very cute name. My name is Linne, but you can call me Auntie if you wish."

"Auntie Linne?"

"That has a nice ring to it. I was told you lost your memories following a monster attack, which you fortunately survived without any injuries. It's good that you can remember your name, at least."

"I remember someone telling me I was a good girl, stroking my hair. She called me Mei."

Tears welled up in Mei's eyes, streaming down her cheeks. She wasn't sad. She felt happy.

"I didn't...lose everything. I still have...what's most important."

"Of course. Now, Mei, why don't you try to go back to sleep? You look like you still need more rest."

Mei did as Linne advised, drifting off to sleep again, comforted by this extraordinary kindness. For the first time in many years, she felt safe.

...For the first time in years? Where had that thought come from?

Had she been attacked by a monster, like Auntie Linne said? All she knew was that she'd been somewhere scary for a very long time, and the

person with the kind voice made all the scary things go away. Someone then brought her to this safe place.

Mei wished she could remember more about her savior besides her voice and the feel of her hand on Mei's head, but even that alone was reassuring.

"Good night…Yui…"

◆

Mei said that out of habit, without realizing. When she was soundly asleep, Linne gently stroked the girl's hair.
"Growing up in that house must have been awful for you, with your Sense Danger skill."
Sense Danger was a rare skill, highly valued by criminals. Grown-ups with this skill were impossible to target, since they could sense danger right away. Young children or babies, though, who didn't yet realize what they were sensing, could be kidnapped.
Growing up in an abusive household would cause Sense Danger to ring alarm bells in the child's mind all the time, and many such children would die from stress and constant fear. Mei survived only thanks to Yui. The bracelet Yui made for her as an amulet, oblivious to the effects imbuing an item with magic could have, wasn't just a nice token of sisterly love, but an amulet.

It was Yui who raised the girl kept captive by her family, with care and love, without knowing she had the Sense Danger skill.
"You don't have to be afraid anymore."

* * *

Mei joined Rodin's household as the daughter of the woman the Nuirs had enslaved. Linne took her under her wing and made a very decent seamstress out of her.

Mei had a fear of spiders, so she couldn't become Yui's apprentice, but Linne had trained her well. Everyone, Yui included, loved the garments she made.

As far as the records go, Mei lived the rest of her life in happiness.

••• **EXCLUSIVE SHORT STORY 1** •••

Playing in the Snow and an Amulet

No sooner had I noticed little white flakes falling from the sky than whole clumps of them started drifting down, covering the entire landscape.

"Snow!"

I jumped out into the garden, where the snow was already thirty centimeters deep.

"So pretty!"

It was as if white rose petals were falling from the sky. I felt giddy with excitement.

"Is this your first time seeing snow, Lady Yui?"

"Yes."

In this life, at least.

"Are you warm enough, Yui?" Argit asked.

I nodded.

"I am. It's…pleasantly cool outside."

Argit and I were wearing matching coats I made, but they were rather thin, designed to look stylish, rather than keep us toasty in wintry weather. Mimachi was dressed in a thick coat with a fur-lined hood.

"Eek! It got so freezing all of a sudden!"

"Is it that cold?"

I cocked my head at her and reached down to touch the snow. In my previous life, I lived in a region with very little snow in winter. I had never seen so much.

I touched it with my bare hands, and it felt a little cold, but not enough to bother me. My fingers didn't even turn red.

It was just like that time at the hot spring.

"My fairies...are protecting me."

"Lady Yui, let's play in the snow! It will be a good way for you to build up strength," said Luroo.

She was wearing only a thin cape over her usual clothes.

"Oh, yes!"

I fell backward onto the snow.

"Lady Yui?!"

I reached for Argit's hand, so that my print in the snow would be unbroken.

"What are you doing, Yui?"

"Leaving a print in the snow!"

"Ha-ha, that's the first thing that comes to your mind?"

Argit helped me up, chuckling.

"Lady Yui! How about making a snowman?"

While I was lying in the snow, Mimachi was busily rolling a large snowball.

"Oh!"

I made a little snowball myself, put it down, and started rolling. I managed to make it nicely round, without picking up any dirt. I rolled it over to Mimachi's snowball, which was twice as big.

Playing in the Snow and an Amulet

"Lady Yui's snowball will be perfect for the snowman's head!"

She lifted it up on top of hers, making a Japanese-style two-tier snowman. Mimachi took care of making its face, but the result was rather disturbing.

"Mimachi...are you really a Terra?"

"Not all Terra are amazing at crafts, you know!" Mimachi yelled with tears in her eyes. "Lady Yui, why don't you make a new face for it? This one was...just to give you an idea of what a snowman is. I can make better ones...sometimes..."

She smoothed the snowman's head over, erasing the face that had looked like a failed attempt at Fukuwarai, a game where you try to complete a picture of a human face blindfolded. I wondered what I should do. Should I try to make a face like what Mimachi did?

"..."

Or I could try something else.

I made more small snowballs and stuck two of them on the snowman's head. I used small acorns for eyes and stuck a third snowball in the middle of the face.

"Oh, look at that! A bear!"

A fourth snowball at the back became its tail. I made a little snow bunny out of the fifth snowball next to the bear.

"No way... Lady Yui made a bear instead of a snowman? And it's super cute!" Mimachi praised me.

My eyes sparkled excitedly.

Making snow bunnies was so much fun. I wanted to make more, and more, and more!

"Um... Lady Yui? Isn't that enough snow bunnies? Hello? Can you hear me?"

* * *

I got wholly absorbed by making my snow bunnies, and when I paused to take a break, I saw that one corner of the garden had a whole army of them.

"It's nice to see Yui enjoying something else besides needlework."

Argit made an igloo and moved half of my bunnies into it. The bear and the bunnies I made immediately around it would soon get buried in the still-falling snow.

"Thank…you…Argit."

"Did you enjoy playing in the snow today?"

I nodded enthusiastically.

We had very heavy snowfall, which covered even Argit's igloo. Even though we could no longer see it, I was happy that he thought to make a temporary shelter for my snow creations.

◆

Argit was relieved to see Yui play blithely in the snow. She looked like a little girl, but mentally was very grown-up. She was never difficult, and her life revolved around her work. She didn't display much emotion, remaining stoically calm almost all the time. An unkind person might say she was like a machine—that she was working, but not living.

"Her life at home really was like this…"

Argit thought it wouldn't hurt for Yui to discover other things which might bring her joy besides sewing.

Argit's first wife had no energy for anything. His second wailed over something constantly. In the past, he did have hope for a happy marriage. He wanted someone he could love. It didn't occur to him that a wife who

could see fairies wouldn't cherish them, and that this in turn would make it impossible for him to love her. It was only after he'd stepped down as king that he found someone he could treasure.

While he was relieved to discover that Yui was an artisan, her single-minded devotion to her work also caused him anxiety. Perhaps he had more in common with his previous wife than he'd like to admit.

"I don't deserve Yui…"

When Schnell told them about the selfish love-stricken prince from his homeland, Argit thought the prince was a fool…but secretly, he was chilled by the realization that if Yui had been born into a respectable, high-rank family and he heard about her back when he was looking to marry for the first time, she too might have angrily rejected him, seeing him as nothing more than an obstruction to her work.

"Argh!"

Argit sunk back into his bed limply.

He'd proposed to Yui in order to guarantee her safety. He'd been planning to find her a man more suitable as a romantic partner later. When Schnell expressed interest in meeting Yui, he introduced them to each other without any objections. Yet he surprised himself by feeling a deep sense of relief when it became clear that there was no trace of romantic attraction between the two, despite them getting along really well as fellow artisans. Argit didn't know if his relief was due to the fact that he'd developed a less than optimistic view of romance and marriage, or whether it was because he wanted Yui all to himself.

Argit didn't tell anyone about these troubling thoughts.

He hoped that a day would come when he'd feel a reassuring certainty that he wouldn't develop romantic feelings for Yui.

◆

The snow bunnies were hopping, some landing deep in the snow. When making the snow bunnies and the snow bear, Yui was imagining how fun it would be if they could come to life, and the world changed accordingly, making her fantasy a reality. One of her bunnies even became an amulet.

From that winter onward, snowmen, snow bunnies, and any other snow animals came to life when nobody was looking.

The bunnies hopped around, playing in the snow. They secretly helped people out, too.

When a person clearing snow away with a shovel was about to lose their balance and fall over, a snow bunny would brush against their feet to steady them.

When someone was about to be buried under an avalanche, it would turn into a giant clump of snow bunnies, which would scatter and disappear.

Yui had no idea about this. She didn't realize she had created another amulet, although she would have if this amulet had been made of thread and fabric.

The first time she made an amulet, that friendship bracelet, she didn't even know what amulets were. She'd learned a lot since then, but she wouldn't have suspected that one of the many snow bunnies she made would also become one.

Two hundred and fifty years later, a little snow divine beast in the form of a snow bunny realized that it began its existence as an amulet.

None of the humans knew that even before Yui created her first fairy through her blessweaving, even before she raised her spider into a divine beast, she gave life to a snow bunny as an amulet, birthing a brand-new divine beast.

EXCLUSIVE SHORT STORY 2

Love at First Sight for a Mermaid

This is a tale from the not-too-distant future.

An adventurer walking with crutches arrived in the city of Menesmetlo. He was of a medium build, with dark navy hair and eyes. His looks were average, with no unusual characteristics which would draw the eye.

He didn't give the impression of an adventurer, in fact, and was often mistaken for an apprentice merchant. The reason he wasn't mistaken for a full-fledged merchant was that he had a trusting, gullible personality.

This apprentice-merchant-like adventurer was called Kokonotsu. He was the second son of struggling farmers, and since he didn't seem too bright when he was a child, he was raised knowing he wouldn't inherit the farm.

What also caused him problems was the fact that he was born with the ability to see water fairies. Faysight was a rare ability—and unlike in the big cities, in the countryside, people often didn't know that some could see the hidden world of fairies. When a water fairy became Kokonotsu's familiar, he'd spend all the time playing with his invisible companion. Others couldn't understand what he was doing and even thought he was creepy.

Aware that his parents would be only too happy to be rid of him, Kokonotsu left his village as soon as he was of an age to do so and became an adventurer. He couldn't find anywhere he'd want to stick around, so he kept wandering from one land to the next, teaming up with any other adventurers who'd approach him to earn some coin.

In the previous country he'd passed through, he joined a group of really decent people. He considered himself lucky to be a member of a party which genuinely valued him, and he in turn cared about them a lot—which is why he threw himself in the line of danger to save the party leader's lover.

Kokonotsu was gravely wounded and almost lost his leg. He thought he'd die from his injuries, but his party members were determined to heal him. They made a healing preparation using ingredients from high-level dungeons, which saved his life and partially healed his leg. Then they used their connections to get him seen by a famous medic, hoping that with the right help, Kokonotsu would make a full recovery. Unfortunately, the medic concluded that Kokonotsu would never recover full use of his injured leg.

Kokonotsu tried to cheer up his despairing comrades by telling them he'd give up the life of an adventurer and try something new, so they need not worry…but of course, they did.

Before meeting them, the naive, gullible Kokonotsu had been taken advantage of by other adventurers, who'd pay him next to nothing for helping them, and by unscrupulous merchants, one of which almost succeeded at making Kokonotsu his slave. Outside of adventuring, he had no skills or talents that could get him work. Even as he was telling his friends not to worry, he was very anxious about his future.

Add to this the fact that he was only eighteen, which was very young

Love at First Sight for a Mermaid

for an adventurer. He didn't look particularly strong, either. Even rookies would try to boss him around.

The only viable option was for him to remain an adventurer. But where could he find work without being automatically rejected due to his appearance and lame leg?

His party kept searching for an answer until they found it. It was the city of Menesmetlo, famous for its hot spring labyrinth. Almost every building was an inn with hot spring access. Many adventurers would travel there in part to recuperate, when not exploring the labyrinth, half of which was a network of canals and underground hot springs. With his high-level water fairy familiar, Kokonotsu would be invincible in water, and his disability wouldn't be a problem.

Kokonotsu had suffered such serious injuries only because that battle took place in the desert, where his familiar couldn't help him. The fairy assisted in another way, though—it was thanks to fairy magic that the medicine Kokonotsu's friends made using expensive labyrinth ingredients turned out to be miraculously effective. Both he and the rest of his party knew that his water fairy must have been very powerful. Gradually, each of the party members acquired a water fairy of their own, no doubt attracted by Kokonotsu's. They got very excited talking about how they would be able to take on quests in the Menesmetlo labyrinth together.

Kokonotsu arrived in the city alone, though, since after purchasing the ingredients for his medicine, the group only had enough funds to cover one person's travel expenses. They sent him on, trying to silence their fears and worries by telling themselves he'd be fine with all the water around.

Incidentally, neither Kokonotsu nor his concerned friends knew that all those who hurt him or tried to swindle him ended up falling victim to floods and then a drought.

* * *

"I'm finally here!"

His muscles stiff from sitting so long in the carriage, Kokonotsu clambered out, taking care not to get in anyone's way. Outside, he stood with his crutches, taking in the beautiful scenery of the city in its spring exuberance.

His friends had treated him, spending all their money on his travel and accommodation. They were planning to join him in a year's time at the earliest, after they'd saved up enough money. Kokonotsu was intent on repaying his debt to them then.

"All right. Let's find the Adventurers Guild..."

A sudden gust of wind made him screw his eyes shut.

"Whoa! Didn't expect blustery weather... Hmm, that reminds me—there's a wind labyrinth here, too."

Scatterings of colorful petals danced in the wind, rising high into the clear blue sky.

"Got to say, this city's beautiful. This whole country is. So many water fairies around."

He glanced at the merman leisurely swimming beside him. The handsome merman carried a trident. On his head, slightly askew to the right, was a coral-reef shaped tiara made of crystal and jade. He seemed livelier since they'd entered this country.

The merman was Kokonotsu's fairy familiar. Little water fairies would drift up to him and greet him, kissing his cheeks covered in rainbow scales. It was adorable.

Another strong gust of wind blew the little fairies away as they chuckled, enjoying it. It seemed as if someone had caught them in the air, and while Kokonotsu couldn't see anything, he guessed it must have been a wind fairy. When the wind stopped, he caught a few falling petals with

Love at First Sight for a Mermaid

a smile, wondering if the wind fairies were playing with flower and plant fairies around him.

"I'm liking this city already... What's that?"

Something else was falling from the sky, much bigger than petals. Kokonotsu instinctively caught it.

"H-huh?"

It was a dainty hat, which must have belonged to a high-born lady. With the thin silk veil, there was no mistake.

Kokonotsu looked around in surprise and saw a lady coming down the street.

"Ah!"

The lady was dressed like a maid. He figured she was looking for her mistress's hat, which had flown away in the strong wind. He held out the hat toward her, and she smiled with relief. Then she looked up from the hat, at him. The moment their eyes met, the ground escaped from under Kokonotsu's feet, and he was plunged into a deep lake... At least, that's how it felt to him. He was still standing on firm ground at the coach station, but he felt as if he were falling, and he couldn't breathe.

The woman's pretty, gentle eyes reflected only Kokonotsu. Even though there was still quite some distance between them, all he could see were her eyes. The part of his brain which managed to remain calm registered that his heart rate was faster than even when he thought he was about to die. Hazily, he remembered overhearing women talking about romance, mentioning falling in love at first sight.

◆

Luroo Loulouoo was a mermaid, and mermaids lived in the sea. They would only come out on land during the estrus, when they were looking for men to mate with. Luroo was an exception in that she left her salty homeland driven by curiosity about life on land, where she became interested in medicine, leading her to become a nurse.

Still, unusual though she might be, she was a mermaid, and it was mermaids' nature to attract men with their beauty so that they could bear children. To humans, it might sound outrageous, but mermaids saw human men as studs for breeding. If they found a good quality mate, they would even share him for reproduction. For the man, it was similar to having a harem of beauties, but it would be them who were the masters. Also, the mermaids wouldn't love the man—his role would be only that of a necessary tool for procreation. Normally, mermaids felt no desire toward men.

Since coming onto the land, Luroo had seen many human women smitten with love. She couldn't understand what that was like. She thought she never would, being a mermaid.

Luroo had been out on a walk with Yui when a playful wind fairy made Yui's hat fly off her head. Had Schnell with his wind fairy king been with them, wind fairies wouldn't dare play tricks like that.

She chased after the hat. A young man caught it. When she met his eyes, for a moment, she forgot about the entire world.

Mermaids didn't normally fall in love, but when they did, it was usually love at first sight.

Luroo's instincts kicked in, focusing her magic in her eyes to charm the man, to not let him get away. She thought she shouldn't be doing this, but her nature was stronger than her. When he reflected her magic back at her, her guilty conscience was relieved.

"Your name... Could you please tell me your name? I'm Luroo."

Love at First Sight for a Mermaid

Without thinking, she introduced herself to the man. But she didn't tell him her mermaid name, Loulouoo. She didn't want to make him her captive, or to share him with the other mermaids. She wanted him to know her only as Luroo, to love him as a woman, not to possess him as a mermaid.

"I'm Kokonotsu."

His voice was like an arrow which pierced her heart. Her ears were burning, thoughts swirling around in her head without her control, which somehow felt so good.

Her instincts told her he would be the one doing the choosing. She suspected that any mermaid would have fallen for him as soon as they saw him, as soon as they heard his voice, and that they, too, would be powerless against him, having to meekly await his acceptance or rejection.

They'd only just exchanged names, but Luroo's chest hurt from the passionate love she could barely contain, and her eyes glistened with tears she was still somehow holding back.

"P-please marry me!" the man stuttered.

"I will!" Luroo shouted back.

His out-of-the-blue proposal was crazy, but so was she, hopelessly love-struck.

◆

A year later, Kokonotsu's friends would arrive in Menesmetlo. He'd have recovered to the point where he no longer needed crutches to walk. They would team up, and their exploits would earn them fame. But first, they would attend Kokonotsu's wedding ceremony. To think that he, who was to them like a little brother, was getting married.

For the time being, his friends were still in faraway lands, worrying whether Kokonotsu was safe and well. They wouldn't have imagined that he'd found the love of his life, proposed to her right off the bat, and that she happily accepted without a moment's thought.

Character Artwork

Character Designs

Yui

••• FIRST OUTFIT •••

Yui was very thin when she arrived at Rodin's residence.

Lots of fabric to cover up as much skin as possible.

The dress fits perfectly even without a corset.

Four to five panniers make the skirt more voluminous.

••• ROYAL BALL DRESS •••

Yui's Spider and Fairies

••• SPIDER •••

Covered in long, fluffy hair.

Fits in the palm of Yui's hand.

••• DARK FAIRY (PURPLE PRINCE) •••

Wears a crown, since he's a fairy king.

His amazing sword can cut thread and remove curses.

••• TREE FAIRY •••

Her hair is semi-transparent, revealing a pattern on the underside.

••• MOONTIDE FAIRY •••

Her mermaid tail is hidden under her dress.

Character Designs

Argit

••• FIRST OUTFIT •••

This cringey getup was made for him by Yui's father.

••• NEW AND IMPROVED OUTFIT •••

Argit's clothes following Yui's alterations. A simple design that highlights his nice physique.

Mimachi

Pearl hairclips add subtle flair.

She'd be such a beauty if only she kept her mouth shut.

••• ORIGINAL DESIGN •••

We also considered having her wear her hair in braids, or having straight, short hair.

Character Designs

Rodin & Endelia

••• RODIN •••

Some of his long hair is in a ponytail.

This intimidating housekeeper is out-of-this-world beautiful.

••• ENDELIA •••

Hania & Amnart

••• HANIA •••

Her dress was made by House Furke seamstresses.

Stiff but kind visage.

A somewhat flashy collar and an open shirt.

••• AMNART •••

Afterword

Hello, everyone!

Can you believe it's been years since the first volume? But that's what you get from Zeroki, the snail-paced writer!

I've caused a lot of trouble for my editor while we worked on getting Volume 2 out. I'm really sorry about that!

I also owe apologies to my patient readers who had to wait such a long time for the continuation of the story! Let me apologize in advance for the next volume also not coming out in a timely manner!

That's it for apologies. Now, about the *Maiden of the Needle* manga! I bet you already know about the ongoing manga adaptation by Yuni Yukimura! It's so cute! So exciting! Wait, it's based on the story I wrote? She presents it in such a fun way that I keep forgetting about it!

Some of you might have picked up the novel after reading the manga, and I'm so happy you did! As you can see now, my books are very clumsy creations compared to Yuni's manga, ha-ha.

In the light novel series, Yui's a super cute girl, but she has the soul of an old artisan, so be warned! There won't be any thrilling romantic developments involving her! For some reason, I thought I should tell you this, so you wouldn't get any ideas based on just how adorable Yui is in the manga.

Miho Takeoka's illustrations are super cute, too! I swoon every time she shows me new ones. She made me want fairy and snow bunny Nendoroids or plushies!

I've actually been up to all sorts of things since my debut, such as selling autographs! But a sheet of paper with just three lonely katakana characters didn't seem right, so I've been adding illustrations of one of the minor fairies from the story. Not the sort of thing a writer should be scribbling on autographed paper, right? Heh… I hope I'll at least be forgiven for how amateurish those drawings look. I'm just a writer, after all!

Next time I do the autographs, I'll draw snow bunnies, a whole lot of them, to fill the page. Or no, wait… Those may actually be hard to draw. I'm not even confident I can draw a proper ellipsis.

Anyway, I'd better focus on writing the next volume, right? This time it won't take me longer than a year, I'm sure… I'm so sorry for not living up to my promise from the first volume's afterword! In any case, I'll try to be faster this time around!

Thank you so much for reading *Maiden of the Needle*, Volume 2!

Illustrated Afterword

Hello! Sorry for only introducing myself now. I'm Miho Takeoka, the illustrator.

My parents were clothiers who made Western-style clothes, so I'm very familiar with the craft of sewing, and I find making clothes more satisfying than wearing them.

When the *Maiden of the Needle* editor approached me asking if I'd be interested in working on a sewing fantasy story, they couldn't have known about that interest of mine. I still don't know why they chose me for this project, but I'm really glad I got to meet Yui and all the other characters from her world through it.

Work on the manga adaptation began during the two years we waited for Zeroki to finish writing the second novel, so I've been busy designing characters on the side. There are so many characters in *Maiden of the Needle*—and so many outfits!

For me (and probably for Zeroki, too), coming up with good ideas takes time. While I don't know when the next volume might come out, I hope you can wait!

miho Takeoka.

HAVE YOU BEEN TURNED ON TO LIGHT NOVELS YET?

86—EIGHTY-SIX, VOL. 1-11

In truth, there is no such thing as a bloodless war. Beyond the fortified walls protecting the eighty-five Republic Sectors lies the "nonexistent" Eighty-Sixth Sector. The young men and women of this forsaken land are branded the Eighty-Six and, stripped of their humanity, pilot "unmanned" weapons into battle…

Manga adaptation available now!

WOLF & PARCHMENT, VOL. 1-6

The young man Col dreams of one day joining the holy clergy and departs on a journey from the bathhouse, Spice and Wolf. Winfiel Kingdom's prince has invited him to help correct the sins of the Church. But as his travels begin, Col discovers in his luggage a young girl with a wolf's ears and tail named Myuri, who stowed away for the ride!

Manga adaptation available now!

SOLO LEVELING, VOL. 1-8

E-rank hunter Jinwoo Sung has no money, no talent, and no prospects to speak of—and apparently, no luck, either! When he enters a hidden double dungeon one fateful day, he's abandoned by his party and left to die at the hands of some of the most horrific monsters he's ever encountered.

Comic adaptation available now!

THE SAGA OF TANYA THE EVIL, VOL. 1-12

Reborn as a destitute orphaned girl with nothing to her name but memories of a previous life, Tanya will do whatever it takes to survive, even if it means living life behind the barrel of a gun!

Manga adaptation available now!

SO I'M A SPIDER, SO WHAT?, VOL. 1-16

I used to be a normal high school girl, but in the blink of an eye, I woke up in a place I've never seen before and—and I was reborn as a spider?!

Manga adaptation available now!

OVERLORD, VOL. 1-16

When Momonga logs in one last time just to be there when the servers go dark, something happens—and suddenly, fantasy is reality. A rogues' gallery of fanatically devoted NPCs is ready to obey his every order, but the world Momonga now inhabits is not the one he remembers.

Manga adaptation available now!

VISIT YENPRESS.COM TO CHECK OUT ALL OUR TITLES AND...

GET YOUR YEN ON!